A Cage Without Bars

A Cage Without Bars

—— *By Anne Dublin* ——

Second Story Press

Library and Archives Canada Cataloguing in Publication

Dublin, Anne, author

A cage without bars / Anne Dublin.

Issued in print and electronic formats.

ISBN 978-1-77260-069-8 (softcover).--ISBN 978-1-77260-074-2
(HTML)

1. Jewish children--Sao Tome and Principe--History--Juvenile

fiction. 2. Child slaves--Sao Tome and Principe--History--Juvenile

fiction. 3. Sao Tome and Principe--History--Juvenile fiction. I. Title.

PS8557.U233C34 2018   jC813'.6   C2018-901631-0

C2018-901632-9

ISBN 978-1-77260-069-8 (softcover)
ISBN 978-1-77260-074-2 (e-book)

Printed and bound in Canada
Text © Anne Dublin
Cover image © Sue Todd
Edited by Carolyn Jackson
Designed by Ellie Sipila

*Second Story Press gratefully acknowledges the support of the
Ontario Arts Council and the Canada Council for the Arts for our
publishing program. We acknowledge the financial support of the
Government of Canada through the Canada Book Fund.*

ONTARIO ARTS COUNCIL
CONSEIL DES ARTS DE L'ONTARIO
an Ontario government agency
un organisme du gouvernement de l'Ontario

Canada Council   Conseil des Arts
for the Arts   du Canada

TORONTO   FUNDED BY
ARTS   THE CITY OF
COUNCIL   TORONTO

Funded by the Government of Canada
Financé par le gouvernement du Canada

Published by
SECOND STORY PRESS
20 Maud Street, Suite 401
Toronto, ON M5V 2M5
www.secondstorypress.ca

This book is dedicated to the millions of people—men, women, and children—who are still enslaved in countless places around the globe.

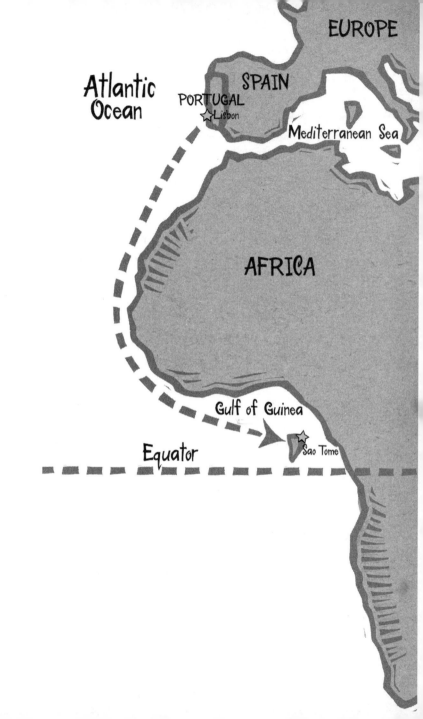

"Fly, thought, on wings of gold!
Go settle upon the slopes and the hills,
where, soft and mild, the sweet airs
of our native land smell fragrant."

"Va pensiero", from "Chorus of the Hebrew Slaves",
Giuseppe Verdi, *Nabucco*, 1842
Lyrics by Temistocle Solera

"... Arriving from the North they cast anchor here
by mandate or by chance in the service of their king:
navigators and pirates
slave traders thieves contrabandists
common folk
also rebel outcasts
and Jewish children
so tender that they faded
like sun-dried ears of corn."

Conceição Lima: "Afro-Insularity",
quoted in Kathleen Becker,
São Tomé and Principe: The Bradt Travel Guide, 2014

HISTORICAL NOTE

For nearly 1,500 years, Jews lived in Spain—for the most part, in harmony with their Muslim and Christian neighbors. But in 1391, conditions began to worsen. Anti-Jewish riots spread throughout Spain, thousands of Jews were killed and thousands more were forced to convert to Catholicism. They were called *conversos*, or New Christians. (People also called them *Marranos*, but that word meant "swine" and was an insult.)

On March 31, 1492, Ferdinand of Aragón and Isabella of Castile, the king and queen of Spain, signed the Edict of Expulsion. One month later, the edict was announced publicly. The monarchs gave the Jews a bitter choice: convert to Catholicism or leave Spain forever. If they did not convert and stayed in Spain, they would be put to death.

Why did the rulers enact such a severe decree? The edict stated that they feared the Jews would influence the conversos to return to Judaism. Also, the monarchs and nobles of Spain wanted to avoid paying the Jews back for the heavy loans they had incurred while waging the recent war to wrest Granada from Muslim control.

Because the Spanish Jews had only three months before they

had to leave—by the end of July—they were forced to sell their homes and possessions at rock bottom prices. Unfortunately, their Christian neighbors profited from the Jews' desperate plight. As one priest wrote:

> Indeed, the Christians took their many estates, rich houses and landed properties for a small amount of money.... They exchanged a house for an ass, and a vineyard for a small piece of cloth or linen, because they could not take out either gold or silver.[1]

It's important to note that any Christians who tried to help the Jews—and some did—risked losing their own possessions. The Edict forbade Christians to "publicly or secretly receive, shelter, or defend any Jew or Jewess...under pain of losing all their property."[2]

Many Jews went overland to nearby Portugal or by sea to Morocco; others to Italy (especially Naples and Ferrara), or to the Ottoman Empire where they were welcomed with open arms.

When approximately 20,000[3] Spanish Jews arrived in Portugal, King João II (John) initially allowed them to enter. After they paid a head tax of eight *cruzados*[4], most of the Spanish Jews had very little to live on. If they couldn't pay, they became slaves of the king or of his nobles.

If the Jews did manage to pay the fee, they were crowded into the *juderia* (Jewish quarter) or in refugee camps. They overwhelmed the resident Portuguese Jews, who felt burdened by this sudden influx of refugees. On their part, the Portuguese Christians, who at that time numbered only about one million, viewed the new arrivals with suspicion.

Portugal was a temporary sanctuary at best. A few relatively prosperous immigrant families were allowed to become permanent residents, but everyone else was required to get out within eight months.

In 1493, the Spanish Jews in Portugal had three choices: leave the country (if they had paid the head tax), become slaves (if they hadn't paid the head tax), or convert to Catholicism. (A few years later, the Jews' *only* choice was to convert.) In the midst of these turbulent events, by order of King João, 2,000[5] Jewish children between the ages of two and twelve were taken from their parents who hadn't paid the head tax, forcibly baptized, and shipped off to the island of São Tomé (Saint Thomas), 150 miles (about 240 kilometers) off the coast of West Africa.

Approximately 600 children survived the sea journey; the rest died of starvation, thirst, disease, and abuse. The survivors were raised as Christians and forced to work on the new sugar plantations. This is the story of those children.

Chapter 1
Trujillo, Spain
1492

I remember well the last Passover I was to celebrate with my family. Everyone was gathered around the table for the *seder*, the special Passover meal: Mother, Father, my younger sister, Gracia, my aunts and uncles and cousins.

Father held up the *matzah*, the unleavened bread, and proclaimed, "Once we were slaves. Now we are free." Then he recounted the story of how the Israelites had been slaves in Egypt. I always looked forward to hearing how Moses led our people to freedom and to the Promised Land. We dipped celery in salt water, we ate matzah and bitter herbs, and we sang our songs of praise to God. "The Lord is with me. I have no fear of what man can do to me."

How I loved the Passover meal! We feasted on leek soup, fish with almond sauce, roast chicken, rice with carrots and lemons, and finally, Mother's famous orange sponge cake.

She and Father had married young, not knowing each other

before marriage, as is our custom. But I had rarely heard a harsh word spoken between them. Father had always worked hard—first as a weaver and later in his textile store. Mother took care of us and our small house.

Only two days later, trumpets sounded and royal heralds assembled the people of the great cities and towns of Spain to hear the Edict of Expulsion, which was to change our lives forever. They announced that by the end of July, every Jew must be gone from the realm. Any Jews who had not left by then would be put to death, unless they became Christians.

The edict was clear; the edict was horrifying. I knew then that for the rest of my life, the sound of trumpets would strike terror deep in my bones.

Everywhere—everywhere I went, everywhere I looked—there was panic, confusion, and despair.

"Isaac, where will we go?" Mother wailed. "What should we do?"

Father stood as if dumbstruck. "I…I will ask Rabbi Judah what to do." He bent down, kissed Mother on the forehead, and hurried out the door.

Mother nodded, but her shoulders shook.

I trembled and held Gracia's hand. She broke away from me and ran into Mother's embrace. "I don't want to go!" she sobbed.

It seemed the world had gone mad. Everything I had always known was now disappearing. I balled my hands into fists. "I won't go. They can't make me!"

"Come here, my son," Mother said. I walked toward her and sank onto the floor at her feet. I admit it. I began to cry. Mother stroked my head. "Whatever happens, we will stay together."

I swallowed my tears. "Do you promise?"

Mother hugged me. "I promise."

When Father returned, new lines had appeared on his face. It seemed to me that he had aged years in that short time.

"What did the rabbi say?" Mother asked.

Father hung his head. "We must leave." His shoulders sagged. "We have no choice unless…"

Mother's eyes widened. "No! We will not become Christians! Never!"

Father put his arm around her shoulders. "Reyna, we will not. I promise you." He sighed deeply. "I will not renounce my faith, and that of my fathers and their fathers before them! No! We will leave Spain. We will find a place in this world where we can practice our religion in freedom."

"And where will that be? Did Rabbi Judah say?"

Father looked away into the distance, as if he could see our destination in his mind. "We shall go to Portugal."

Mother shook her head and her lips trembled. "Portugal? So far away?"

Father sank down into a chair and ran his fingers through his hair. "Rabbi Judah says the other places we might go—North Africa, Italy, the Ottoman Empire—are even farther away and we would have to go by sea."

"But how will we travel?" Mother wrung her hands. "The roads are dangerous, filled with robbers and scoundrels."

"The rabbi says we will go together. Perhaps…that will keep us safe."

Mother looked at Father with tears welling in her deep brown eyes. She took a shaky breath. "Husband, I shall go where you think is best." She brushed wisps of stray hairs (did I see gray?) that had escaped from the tight bun at the nape of her neck.

Father held out his arms. "Come, children." We ran into his arms. "As long as we are together, all will be well."

Father swallowed hard. "After all," he continued, "surely the customs and language of Portugal will be familiar to us. And who knows?" he added, "Even though we will be allowed to stay in Portugal for only eight months, perhaps after that the Spanish monarchs will change their minds, and we will be able to return to our homes here." But in Father's eyes, I did not see hope. Only fear and despair.

Father sold our house and most of our possessions. The money he received in payment was hidden away in the small purse Mother kept beneath her clothes. We were not permitted to take gold or silver out of the country on pain of death. Father packed some linen, wool, and silk, for he hoped to find work in neighboring Portugal.

Mother and Father were busy packing and arranging for our departure. They kept saying time was passing too quickly, but to me it seemed that everything had slowed down, as if I were swimming against a strong tide.

I walked along the familiar cobblestone streets of our town. I recognized every house, every tree, every flower. In my heart, I was saying good-bye to each and every object. I tried to silence the voice in my head: *The last time. The last time. The very last time.* And *It's not fair! It's not fair!*

I clenched my fists, anger boiling deep inside me. I wanted to strike out at something, anything.

All along the streets of the Jewish quarter, people were calling, shouting, crying, arguing. They were packing their belongings in baskets and boxes, trying to load as much as they could onto carts or wagons; trying to exchange their Spanish homes and land for the paltry goods they were allowed to take with them.

Our bags were packed; the donkey loaded. Father locked the door to the house where our family had lived for generations. He stared at the key, sighed deeply, and put it in his pocket.

Then he took a chisel and pried the *mezuzah* off the doorpost. Only its hollowed outline remained. I shivered, for it seemed like a phantom of our family that had lived in this house for so long.

Father kissed the mezuzah. He held it in the palm of his hand and stared at it. He beckoned for me to come closer.

"Yes, Father?"

He had a strange look on his face. "Joseph, you will soon be of bar mitzvah age." He sighed and his shoulders slumped. "I don't know what will await us in faraway Portugal. Maybe good. Maybe bad." He held the mezuzah out to me. The olive wood, worn down by thousands of touches, glowed a warm brown. "Take this mezuzah. Guard it. Maybe it will protect you and give you good luck." Father fingered the tiny piece of parchment inside the case. "My son, always remember the words: 'Hear, O Israel, the Lord is our God, the Lord is One. You shall love the Lord your God with all your heart, with all your soul, and with all your might. And these words which I command you today shall be upon your heart.'"[6]

My hand trembled as I grasped the mezuzah and put it into my pocket. For the rest of our journey, every time I held the mezuzah, I felt its weight and its warmth. It was as if the words were indeed carved into my heart.

Chapter 2

We traveled by foot while our donkey carried what was left of our possessions: pots and pans, dishes and food, clothing and bedding, along with the cloth that Father hoped to sell to start a new business. When Gracia got tired, Father carried her or put her on the donkey.

The donkey was not pleased with his heavy load. We named him Ferdinand (in whispers), for Father said, "The donkey is stubborn and wants his own way." He lowered his voice and added, "Just like King Ferdinand and Queen Isabella, who refuse to allow us to remain in Spain."

Father patted Ferdinand the donkey on the neck. "But you, my fine friend, you will carry us to our new home."

Ferdinand looked at Father as if he understood. He nodded and brayed loudly. When we stopped in the evenings, Father tied him to a tree or large bush. Ferdinand munched on the grass, slept in the shade of the tree, and the next day continued to carry his load.

At night, we slept on blankets on the hard ground by the side of the road. The sky was dark. The moon was hidden and did not light our way. It seemed that even the heavens conspired against us.

We walked—Mother, Father, myself, and Gracia. We walked day after day after day along endless roads in the bruising summer heat. We were afraid to stop for fear we would not be out of Spain by the deadline. The soles of my shoes were worn thin as paper; my feet were blistered and sore. But still we walked.

We walked along with thousands of other exiles—the young, the old, the healthy, the sick; men, women, and children. Women gave birth; old people died; small children sickened. But still we walked.

On the way, we ate bread, cheese, sardines, olives, dried fruit, and nuts. We drank water and ate oranges when we could get them. I missed the delicious soups and stews that Mother had cooked. I remembered that last Passover meal and my mouth watered with longing and yes, with greed.

At most of the villages we passed, the local priest waved his crucifix, clutched his Bible, and shouted, "Convert, you Jews! Christ died for your sins! You will be assured a place in heaven if you give up your old religion and become Christians!"

Some villagers shouted insults like, "Good riddance!" or "We should have done this a long time ago" or "Christ killers!" Others threw rotten fruit and vegetables at us, or even clods of earth or stones.

Father pursed his lips, Mother lowered her head, and we plodded on. My stomach churned, but I gritted my teeth and refused to cry.

Gracia sobbed and hid her face in Mother's skirts. Mother kept saying, "Do not cry, my jewel. Soon we will come to our new home. All will be well." But Gracia kept crying, the tears running down her grimy cheeks.

At other times, we met villagers who gazed at us with sorrow and offered us bread or figs. Father refused, but Mother accepted the food, saying, "Gracias" each time. She muttered, "I will not let my children starve." Father did not reply.

We tramped over the hot, dusty roads of the Spanish plateau, slept beside small rivers, and climbed up and through the mountains. Finally, we reached the border between Spain and Portugal at the town of Vilar Formoso.

It was then that Ferdinand stopped in his tracks. As much as Father tried, he could not persuade Ferdinand to continue. Father turned his back to us and his body shook, as if he were crying. *But that's impossible*, I thought. *Father never cries.*

I walked closer to Father. "What shall we do?"

He only shook his head.

I looked at Ferdinand and he stared back at me with his deep brown eyes. "Ferdinand must be a Spanish donkey."

"What?" Father said. "What do you mean?"

"He's a Spanish donkey," I said. "He doesn't want to leave Spain, either."

Father took a big breath and let it out slowly. "He doesn't have a choice. Neither do we."

He walked over to Ferdinand and stroked him on the neck. I heard him say, "Come, you stubborn donkey. When we get to

Portugal, I will feed you the sweetest grass you have ever tasted. And perhaps a carrot or an apple as well."

Ferdinand pricked up his ears as if he understood Father, and we continued on our way. Ferdinand, the Spanish donkey, was about to become Ferdinand, the Portuguese donkey.

The border guards stared at the thousands of Jews waiting to cross. "By order of good King João," they shouted, "each Jew must pay eight *cruzados* to enter our country! If you cannot pay, you must turn back or become slaves to the king."

"I do not want to be a slave!" Gracia cried.

"Nor do I." My heart was pounding. The soldiers seemed fearsome to me with their swords and helmets, with their hard eyes and fierce scowls.

Mother clutched Father's arm. "Isaac, that is all our savings. To the last coin!"

"We must pay it. How else can we cross the border to safety?"

"Safety?" Mother snorted. "There is no safety for us. Anywhere."

Father put his arm around Mother's shoulders. "Reyna, we must not despair. Think of the children."

Mother gazed at us. "Yes. Always." She turned her back to us, pulled out her small purse from under her clothes, and handed the purse to Father. "We will pay the money." She balled her hands into fists. "My children will never become slaves."

Father paid the head tax, muttering, "They bleed us for everything we have. First the Spanish, now the Portuguese."

My head was filled with worries. How could we live without

any money? How would we find a place to live? How would we pay for food? And what would happen after the eight months were over? Where would we go then? But I kept my worries to myself. I did not want to burden my parents, or upset Gracia more than she was already. I tried to act like a grown-up, but inside I felt as helpless as a baby.

The guards told us to go to the city of Lisbon. They said the Jews who lived in the *juderia* would take care of us. After another three days' journey, we finally arrived in Lisbon, the biggest city I had ever seen. And what a noise and clamor greeted us there!

The city was a jumble of streets, going every which way. At the top of a hill was the grand palace where we were told the king lived. The main street, New Merchants Street, was packed with shops of all kinds—booksellers, hat and cloak makers, apothecaries, silk workshops. There were so many that they made my head spin!

After the clean air of the plateau and the mountains, the smells of the city hit my nostrils like a giant wave—fish, meat, fruit, vegetables, spices, old clothes—all mixed together in a disgusting stew. But worst of all was the stink of the contents of chamber pots thrown out of windows. Several times, we had to hurry past or be sprayed with the reeking contents.

I gagged and vomited the contents of my breakfast by the side of the road.

The Jews in the juderia were overwhelmed by our numbers and most bitterly resented our presence. As we plodded through their streets, I could hear them talking.

"We can hardly feed ourselves," one woman complained. "How can we take care of so many poor people?"

"Where will they live?" another said. "We are crowded enough already!"

"They will take away our jobs and our livelihood," one man grumbled.

"Don't worry so much," said another. "They'll be gone in eight months. The king promised. Then things will be back to normal."

"And if they aren't?" said the first man.

The second man shrugged. "What choice will we have? We Jews have always taken care of our own. The Torah says it is a *mitzvah*, a commandment, to welcome the stranger."

"But so many?"

Father managed to find a room in the juderia. We shared a kitchen with three other families, but it felt wonderful to finally have a roof over our heads. He soon found work in a weaver's shop, and earned enough money to pay for our room and food.

During that time, Gracia started acting younger than the ten-year-old she was. She followed Mother everywhere. At night, she held her cloth doll to her chest and talked to her as if she were a real person. I often put my hands over my ears to block out her foolish words.

Before we came to Lisbon, I had had little to do with Gracia. I had been busy with my schoolwork and playing with my friends—especially David, the rabbi's son. Gracia had stayed home with Mother, learning the things that girls are supposed to learn. Mother often praised Gracia for her sewing, saying she had much talent with the needle.

But things changed when we were uprooted from our home. At times, I played with Gracia to keep her company and to try to forget the home we had left behind; at other times, I resented her girlish ways and lost patience with her.

"Why do you always play with your stupid doll?" I complained, after the hundredth time she wanted to play "house" and pretend I was Father and she was Mother.

Gracia would pout, and her lips would tremble. "She's *not* a stupid doll." Then she would pound on my chest with her fists. "Take it back! Take it back!" she would shout. "You're the worst brother in the world! I hate you!"

Mother would come running from the kitchen. Pulling Gracia away from me, she would say, "What is the matter with you children? Don't I have enough worries without you squabbling all the time?"

We would quiet down then. I would read a story to Gracia or take her for a walk down to the harbor. We were like tender shoots that had been pulled up from the rich earth. Where would we be planted now?

Sometimes at night, I would get up from my bed and look out the window. I would stare at the twinkling stars in the black velvet sky and wonder if these were the same stars that were shining over Spain. I would stand there, the tears streaming down my face.

The stars soon lost their brightness as dark night descended upon us.

Chapter 3
Lisbon, Portugal
1493

Time seemed to stretch and contract during those eight months in Portugal. I was often confined to my Hebrew lessons in a stuffy classroom. I tried to pay attention to the words of the teacher, but the lessons seemed to go on forever. I felt restless all the time. My body would twitch, as if it had a mind of its own. The sky was so blue then; the air filled with birdsong and the scent of flowers.

But I knew that it had been hard for Father to pay for my lessons. I also feared the stick that the teacher used on our palms or knuckles when our attention strayed. But oh, it was hard. I could not concentrate on my studies when there was so much to explore in this new land!

When I was finally released and was playing in the narrow, winding alleyways of the juderia or among the makeshift stalls in the market or along the river with my friend, David, time passed quickly, like the river rushing to the sea.

One night, when they thought I was sleeping, I heard Mother and Father whispering.

"Husband," Mother asked, "what will we do when the eight months have passed? Where will we go?"

There was a long pause. I could hear Father sigh heavily. "I will ask my cousin Moises in Antwerp to send us money for our passage. We must trust in God that all will be well."

"I am so afraid," Mother said.

"Reyna, try not to worry. We must be strong for the children."

"Yes. For the children."

"In the meantime, we must wait and see."

Several weeks later, Mother and Father decided to go north to the city of Antwerp, in the Lowlands. Father's cousin, Moises, had moved there three years earlier and had started a business in spices. He sent money for our ship's passage. We would join him there.

I wondered what it was like in Antwerp. I imagined it was cold and gray, with heavy rain constantly pelting down on the roofs of the houses. I worried about learning a new language, too. I was just starting to feel comfortable in Portuguese. How would I learn Dutch, a language that was so different from the ones I knew?

"We have no choice," Father said several days before our departure. "If we wish to remain Jews and practice our faith, we must leave Portugal."

Mother shuddered. "So many of our people..." She lowered her eyes. She must have been thinking of her brother, Simon. "So many were forced to become Christians."

"That will not happen to us." Father gestured to me to sit on his lap. "Come here, my son."

I was surprised. It had been years since I had sat on Father's lap. I scrunched down small. I felt comforted, safe, calmer than I had for a long time.

Father patted my head and kissed me on the cheek. "You are growing up, Joseph. Twelve years old already." He hugged me tightly and raised my chin with his finger. His expression seemed to contain sorrow, joy, pride—all at the same time. "Whatever happens to you, I know you will be a strong, brave boy."

I swallowed hard. "I will try."

"Be of good courage and have faith in God. Then all will be well." Father paused. "Do you still have the mezuzah?"

"Yes, Father." I reached into my pocket and felt the familiar hardness of the mezuzah he had given me months ago. *Will it give me courage?* I wondered. *Will it keep me safe?*

Gracia tugged on Father's sleeve. "What about me?" She raised her chin. "I can be brave, too."

"Gracia doesn't need to be brave," I said. "She's only a girl."

Mother smiled. "Of course, she must be brave."

I heard Father say under his breath, "As do we all in these dark times."

Father had booked passage on a ship to take us from Lisbon to Antwerp. On the morning of our departure, each of us carried a small pack of clothing and food for the journey. Father had sold Ferdinand the donkey to a Portuguese Jew, who promptly changed the donkey's name to Manuel.

As we walked along the narrow streets that led into the main square, more and more of our fellow Jews joined us until a large crowd milled at the entrance to the harbor. I heard people murmuring names of places where they were planning to go—places I had only seen on an old map that Rabbi Judah had once shown us: Morocco, Naples, Ferrara, the Ottoman Empire. The places sounded strange to my ears, even exciting.

Many ships, large and small, were anchored far out in the harbor. Their sails flapped gaily in the breeze. The sun sparkled on the water and gulls screeched above our heads. I thought then that we were setting out on a great adventure. I was soon to be proven wrong.

Rabbi Judah stood in front of us and chanted, "Moses said, 'Do not be afraid, my people. Do not despair. Let us remember the miracles of God on high. He is one; there is no other. He is Master of all the world.'"[7]

"Now would surely be a good time for a miracle," Father whispered.

Mother's shoulders were shaking. "Are we always to be outcasts? Feared and hated because of who we are?"

"No, dear wife," Father said. "Somewhere we will find a place where we can practice our religion in peace and safety. And then—"

Father was interrupted by loud shouts, the hoofbeats of horses, and the pounding of soldiers' boots.

The bishop, dressed in a black cassock over which he wore a fine cloak of red and purple, led a line of priests carrying crosses and Bibles. Soldiers armed with spears and swords pushed us together until we were hemmed in on three sides. Our backs were to the sea.

I stared at the soldiers, then at the priests, then at the ships in the harbor and the longboats near the shore. My breath came in short gasps. I huddled next to Father. I felt as if I were choking.

The bishop walked toward us and waved his gold crucifix. "This is your last chance! Convert now and be saved!"

Everyone was silent, but then Rabbi Judah stepped forward. "You tell us to convert? We have endured exile from Spain and a grueling journey to this country. Why would we give up now when we are ready to leave again?"

One of the priests shoved the rabbi aside. He stumbled and almost fell onto the hard stones. My friend David reached out and helped his father stand upright.

"Abandon your false faith!" the bishop shouted. His face was red and his hand was shaking as he held up his crucifix. The sun shone on it, but I shut my eyes against its harsh glare.

Here and there, I heard whispers of *"Shema Israel"* or the whimpers of children. My feet felt glued to the ground.

For the third time, the bishop raised his crucifix. "Come to the one true faith! Be saved now!"

Someone in the crowd said, "Let us go now!"

Another said, "The king promised us safe passage!"

The bishop waved these protests away, as if we were nothing but pesky flies. "You are slaves of the king now," he said. "He has his own plans for you." He smirked. "As do I."

Rabbi Judah stepped forward again and raised his hand. The crowd fell silent. He stared at the bishop and, in a shaking voice, said, "Please. Can you not let us go? Even Pharaoh in Egypt let the Israelites go."

The bishop snorted. "Yes. Only after the Egyptians were struck down with the plagues! Do you have such power now?"

Rabbi Judah turned his palms up. "We are only poor people who want to leave this country in peace."

"And why?" The bishop curled his lips. "To practice your false faith somewhere else?" He turned toward the soldiers and shouted, "Take him away!"

A soldier stepped forward, grabbed Rabbi Judah by the arms, and dragged him away.

"No!" His cry was stopped in midair. I could not see what happened, but the rusty smell of blood came to my nostrils. I felt sick to my stomach.

I heard the tramp of soldiers' boots and the clank of metal coming closer, closer. At first, I could not see what was happening, but I heard the wails of women, the cries of children, the shouts of men. My heart raced and the sweat poured down my face.

Father put his arms around Gracia and me. "Hold on to me," he said through gritted teeth. "No matter what happens."

We clutched Father's arms—me on his right, Gracia on his left. Mother stood behind us. I could feel her trembling hand on my shoulder and smell the sweat from her body. My legs were shaking so hard I could barely stand.

A burly soldier pushed people aside as he approached us. "What do we have here?" he barked. "Two little chicks ready to be plucked!"

He raised his spear and knocked Father down onto the hard stones. Father collapsed in a heap. The soldier grabbed Gracia and me and pulled us away from Mother's grasp.

"Mother!" I cried. The soldier smacked my mouth hard and I tasted blood.

"No!" Mother screamed. "Joseph! Gracia!"

I glanced back. Mother was down on her knees, her arms outstretched, tears running down her cheeks.

The soldier tossed me to another soldier, and then another, until I was thrown onto the beach along with the other children. I searched frantically through the wall of soldiers that separated us from our parents. Sand was in my eyes, in my shoes, between my toes. My mouth was so dry I could not speak.

I held tightly to Gracia's hand, and she held mine. I felt as if someone were playing a cruel game of hide-and-seek with us. We had been found and now were being punished. *What will they do to us?* Everything seemed to swirl around me in a chaotic jumble of sounds and images.

Gracia gripped her doll and gazed at me with tear-filled eyes. "Joseph? What's happening?"

But what could I say? What did I know? I could not answer. I could not make sense of anything.

All around me, children were crying and wailing for their parents. Some had accidents and their clothes smelled of urine—or worse. Snot ran down their noses and tears down their cheeks. Some lay on the sand, curled up tightly in a ball.

Some children were as young as two years old—scarcely out of babyhood and diapers. We sat and waited. We waited for we knew not what. The sun blazed down upon our heads. My mouth was parched and my stomach was churning.

The priests came. They sprinkled their holy water on each of us. "In the name of the Father, the Son, and the Holy Ghost, know that Jesus Christ died for your sins. Now you are and will always be Catholic, the one true faith."

As the drops landed on my head, I expected that each one would feel like a burning coal. They did not. It was water. Only water.

When the priests had finished, the soldiers forced us down to the shoreline. They struck us on the heads or backs to make us hurry. They hauled us up if we tripped. They pushed us into the longboats.

The sailors in the boats watched all these happenings without expression, as if we were nothing but their usual cargo of figs or oranges.

I found myself in the same boat as my friend, David. He had a purple bruise on his forehead. His left eye was puffy and swollen.

"What happened to you?" I whispered.

David touched his forehead and winced. "One of the soldiers didn't like my attitude." His voice was choked. "When…when I tried to help my father." He tried to brush the blood-caked hair out of his eyes. "I don't know where they're taking us, but I have a feeling it's no place good."

I nodded. "Me too." I looked back at the city nestled among its hills and the river Tagus flowing into the ocean. I was afraid that I would never see this place again; that I would never see my parents again.

The vomit rose up my throat. I leaned over the side of the boat. I heaved until my stomach felt empty.

When the boats moved away from the harbor, a great wail arose from our parents, crying out our names.

"Isaac!"

"David!"

"Reuven!"

"Gracia!"

"Joseph!"

"Shimon!"

Their cries grew fainter and fainter as we were rowed toward the three-masted ships waiting at anchor. I had seen many of these carracks when I'd played near the harbor with my friends, but never did I imagine I would travel on one without my parents.

The sound of our parents' voices blended with the shrieks of seagulls and were soon lost in the wind and the waves. Forever lost.

Chapter 4

They did not need ropes or chains to restrain us. We were bound by our grief and terror.

We older children were prodded up rope ladders, as if we were nothing but a herd of goats. The sailors carried the little ones on their backs or under their arms. They dropped them onto the deck without a care for bruises or broken bones. A line of soldiers stood on guard on the deck—as if we would try to escape. What could we do? Where could we go?

I rushed up to the sailor who was carrying Gracia over his shoulder. He glanced at me as he put Gracia down.

Her eyes were brimming with tears; her body trembled as if she had the palsy. I was uncertain about what to do. Mother had always been there to comfort us if we were sick or hurt.

I knelt down and put my arms around her. Gracia clutched my shirt and clung close to me.

"Don't worry. I'll make sure she's all right," the sailor said.

I couldn't believe what the sailor was saying. To hear those few kind words from a stranger brought a lump to my throat.

"My name's Luis." He squinted at me in the searing glare of the midday sun. He patted Gracia on the head but she buried her face against my chest. "Maybe you and this girly here will make it."

"Why do you care?" I felt myself turning red. I remembered how Father had always insisted on courtesy and good manners.

The sailor looked about warily, leaned toward me, and hissed, "That's my business. Not yours."

I stared at this short, muscular man. In spite of his brusque words, I thought I saw kindness in his eyes, and perhaps sorrow as well. My heart skipped a beat. *Can there be some hope here after all?*

"Where are they taking us?" I said. "Do you know?"

Luis glanced over his shoulder. "You'll find out soon enough." He lowered his voice. "What's your name?"

"Joseph. This is my sister, Gracia."

Luis nodded. "Just watch out for the first mate. He's a bad one. You'll know him by his pockmarked face." With these words, he disappeared over the side of the ship—probably to haul another child up onto the deck.

"Come on, Gracia," I said. "Let's find a place to sit down."

Gracia shook her head and buried it deeper against my chest. "I don't understand," she said in a muffled voice.

I grabbed her shoulders and made her look at me. "Remember what Father said?"

"What?"

"You must be strong and brave." My legs were shaking but I tried not to show Gracia how afraid I really was.

She kicked at a wooden plank on the deck with the toe of her shoe. "I don't *want* to be strong! I want to go home." She looked up at me. "You'll think I'm a baby."

"No. I won't. Not ever again."

She hung her head. "I lost my doll."

I stared at the sailors bringing more children onto the deck of the ship. It seemed there were hundreds and hundreds of us—more than I could count. I put my arms around Gracia. "I'm sorry about your doll. We can't go home, Gracia. Not now."

"When?"

"I don't know."

All around me, I heard cries of "Mother! Father!"

The soldiers hemmed us in on all sides. Behind the soldiers stood a friar wearing a white robe and black cape. He was plain-looking, tall and thin. I shuddered when I looked at him. He made me think of a ravenous black bird, ready to pounce on a helpless mouse. Indeed, the Grand Inquisitor of Spain, Tomás de Torquemada, was one of these Dominican friars. Many a time I had heard Father speak of him with despair and loathing.

The friar was muttering something to himself, but I could not hear what he was saying. Maybe it was one of those Christian prayers he would force us to learn. I gritted my teeth and put my hand into my pocket. I clutched my mezuzah until I felt my heart slow down.

Behind the friar stood a group of sailors who wore a motley collection of loose-fitting pants and shirts. I spied Luis among them, but he stood back, as if he didn't want to be noticed. The sailors scowled at us, or looked back toward the harbor or out to sea. I wondered if they wanted to be there even less than we did.

Suddenly, I heard the clanking of metal, and the soldiers stood at attention. Above us, on a raised platform, stood an imposing figure. The man had a high forehead, a thin nose, a trim beard and mustache streaked with gray. A knee-length cloak covered a vest of armor, and a knife in a jeweled scabbard hung from his belt. But what I noticed most were his sharp brown eyes—as if he could look right inside me. I admit it. I stepped back.

Immediately, there was a hush. Only a few children hiccupped or whined now. Everyone from the youngest to the oldest must have realized that this man, this captain, held their lives in his hands.

I was standing near the front and saw the captain beckon to the friar who hurried over to his side. In a low voice, the captain said, "Friar Escobar, what did the king mean by this?"

Friar Escobar clutched the gold cross hanging from a heavy chain around his neck. "Captain, perhaps the king thought the Spanish Jews would convert if threatened with the loss of their children. If they converted, he would allow them to stay in Portugal."

"Or if they had paid the head tax, they would still be free."

But Father paid the tax! I wanted to protest.

The captain narrowed his eyes. "But they did not become Christians. And now, instead of the one hundred African slaves he promised, the king has given me these useless Jewish brats." He shook his head. "Never mind. After we land, I shall purchase slaves from the Guinea coast. As for these—"

"But, Captain! They are baptized now. They will be raised as Christians."

The captain frowned. "Nevertheless, I will need strong slaves to work the sugar—not a pack of sniveling children!" He waved his hand in dismissal. "Now go!"

The friar slunk away, but I saw a flash of anger in his eyes.

The captain stared at us children crowded on the deck below him. "I am Captain-Major Álvaro Caminha," he announced. "We are embarking on a long voyage. What our destination is, you will find out in good time.

"Meanwhile, I expect you to follow orders. You will eat what you are given. You will sleep where you are told. Theft will not be tolerated aboard my ship."

He gestured to a man who was standing nearby. He had greasy black hair, a pockmarked face, and small, beady eyes. "My first mate, Dom Gomez, will be in charge of your care and of the provisions for the journey. You will find that he is a man of little patience." Caminha waved us away. "Take them below."

Gomez stepped forward. "Yes, Captain!"

With the help of the soldiers, Gomez pushed us down a narrow, ladder-like staircase into the hold of the ship. We were crammed onto large, unfinished planks of wood—as if we were sardines lined up on a table at the market, ready to be bought and eaten. They closed the hatch door and left us lying there in the gloom.

It had been hours since we had been snatched from our parents. The hold was so hot, I thought I would suffocate. Although there were a few holes on the sides of the ship above the water line, scarcely a breath of air moved. What there was felt as if it had been breathed ten thousand times over—filled with damp, sweat, and vomit.

Gracia had not let go of me the whole time. I put my arm around her and she snuggled against my chest. All around me, children were crying, sobbing, wailing. Then I remembered a lullaby Mother had sung to Gracia and me when we were small.

Nani, nani,
Nani kere el ijo,
El ijo de la madre,
De chiko se aga grande.
Ay, ay durmite mi alma
Ke tu padre viene
Kon muncha alegria.

The baby wants a lullaby,
Mother's little boy—
He will grow up tall.
Ay, go to sleep my love,
For your father will come soon,
With such happiness.[8]

Some of the children began to hum the tune and a few even sang the words with me. I did not know what the future would hold. I only knew that this song was a comfort and a reminder of home.

Chapter 5

I eventually drifted off to sleep. It was to be only a short respite.

"Up! Up!" a gruff voice shouted. "Time to eat!"

I shook Gracia's arm but she only whimpered, "You're hurting me!"

"Gracia, please!" I tried to pull her to her feet. "Let's climb out of this stinking hole and get some air."

"All right." She pushed my hand away. "But first I have to pee."

"Hold your nose."

"Hmph!" She stomped off to the corner where the sailors had placed a large "necessary" bucket.

"Up!" the voice repeated. "Get up on deck!"

We all clambered up the narrow staircase, the older children helping the younger ones. I staggered through the opening and blinked as the sunlight hit me like a slap across the face.

On one end of the deck, far from where we were being herded together, a group of well-dressed men and women stood staring and pointing at us. They frowned and held handkerchiefs to their noses. *Who are those people?* I wondered. *Why do they look at us as if we're some kind of vermin?*

"Line up, and be quick about it!" Gomez barked.

On each side was a wall of soldiers. We were forced to walk between them.

"In lines—two by two!"

I grabbed Gracia's hand and we inched our way forward.

A sailor handed each of us a metal bowl and spoon. "Take care of these," he muttered. "You'll not get another."

Two huge kettles stood on the deck. A short, fat man wearing a grease-stained apron stood behind one, a ladle held in his pudgy hand. Behind the other kettle stood a boy who seemed to be about my age. He had a sullen look in his eyes. Specks of food were lodged in his greasy hair.

"You'll get fed twice a day," Gomez said. "Eat what you're given and no complaints."

The cook's boy spooned some rice into my bowl. The cook plopped a ladle of something resembling soup on top of it. The liquid was thin and watery, with greasy lumps of vegetables and meat I couldn't recognize. *Is it pork?* I was afraid to ask.

I gagged, but managed to say, "Come, Gracia. Let's find a place to sit down."

Along with a pack of other children, we squeezed under the longboat that hung just above the deck alongside the ship's rail.

Gracia wrinkled her nose. "Ugh! That soup smells disgusting." She put her bowl down and crossed her arms over her thin chest. "I won't eat it!"

"You have to eat," I pleaded. "Try one bite."

But Gracia turned away from me and wrapped her arms around her bent legs. "It makes me want to vomit."

"Please, Gracia!"

"No!"

I stared at the congealing mess in my bowl, scooped up a spoonful, held my breath, and swallowed. The greasy concoction slid down my throat, but then—just as fast—rose up. I rushed to the side of the ship and vomited. Gracia glanced at me with an I-told-you-so look.

I was not the only one. All along the deck, other children were vomiting up the food.

"Your face looks green," Gracia said.

I felt too sick to answer.

Thankfully, the soldiers let us stay on the deck. Most of us were sick from the rolling of the ship on the open sea.

I heard one sailor say, "It's better they vomit over the side of the ship instead of below decks where I'd have to clean up the mess."

"These Jewish pups can't do any harm," one of the soldiers said. "They're too sick to try anything." He shook his head. "I'll be glad when we can put them back down in the hold, though. It's getting too crowded up here."

I couldn't stop yawning and shivering. I lay down where I was and could scarcely move. Everything spun round and round. I vomited until I could vomit no more. Gracia stayed huddled near me. I felt her hand stroking my head as she tried to comfort me.

When I felt my worst, a shadow stood over me. "Look at the horizon, boy. That'll help." It was Luis, the sailor who had carried Gracia up onto this infernal ship.

I hardly had the strength to nod. After that, I tried looking at the horizon and my seasickness gradually faded away. I should have felt grateful, but I felt the opposite. At least while I was sick, I was unaware of what was happening around me. Now that I felt better, everything came into focus.

Hundreds of children were sprawled on the deck in various positions of helplessness. They moaned and cried out. Gracia surprised me, for she tended not only to me but also to the other children lying under the longboat.

Finally, I began to feel more like myself. At the morning meal, I managed to swallow the mush of cooked beans and to keep it down. Now I began to wonder what had happened to my friend David. I was soon to find out.

The soldiers hadn't forced us to go below decks as seasickness swept among us, but now they began to pick us off and made us descend into that foul place. Gracia and I managed to stay under the longboat—as it turned out, a choice location. From there, we had some shade from the hot sun and we could catch a breath of fresh air. We were also less conspicuous to the soldiers and sailors, who liked to torment us by tripping us or bumping into us or calling us "Jewish pigs."

At midday on that third day, when the sun was at its highest and the air scarcely moved, I heard a commotion. Two soldiers were dragging what looked like a bundle of rags up to Captain Caminha, who stood on the platform, his feet apart, his hands on his hips, a frown on his face.

A well-dressed lady stood beside the captain. She was not a pretty woman—her nose was too long and her lips too thin. She wore a hooped dress of dark silk and carried herself with assurance. I knew at once that this was a woman whom one did not oppose.

One of the sailors whispered, "That's the captain's wife, Dona Maria."

Another said, "I wonder why she finally came up on deck?"

The first sailor smirked. "Probably to see the fun."

One of the soldiers saluted. "Sir, here's the boy you were looking for."

The captain stared. "Boy, look at me."

The bundle of rags was David. The bruise on his forehead had turned a sallow yellow. His eye was still half-closed.

"I understand that you have been curious about the provisions on this ship."

"Yes, but—"

"Silence!" Captain Caminha raised his hand. "When I wish you to speak, I will tell you." His gaze swept over the crowd of children who were cowering on the deck, the soldiers standing at attention, the sailors scattered on the deck and up in the rigging, and the ladies and gentlemen clustered at one end of the ship.

He raised his chin and exhaled slowly. "I do not need any children scurrying about the pantry like mice looking for a morsel of cheese." He paused. "On the first day, you were told you would be given food twice a day. I expect you to eat it. Without complaints."

He gestured toward David. "This boy, this *Jewish* boy, thinks he is better than everyone else. That he deserves *special* food." Now the captain looked at the cook. "What, exactly, did he steal?"

The cook's face turned even redder than usual. "Some bread and cheese. Right under my nose."

"And olives, too," piped up the cook's boy.

The captain looked grim. "What do you say to that, boy?"

"I…I couldn't eat the food."

"And what's wrong with it?" sputtered the cook. "I've been cooking on this ship for three years. No one's ever complained before."

I doubted that, but I dared not say a word. The captain raised his hand to silence the cook.

David hung his head and whispered something.

"Speak up, boy," snapped Captain Caminha.

David raised his head. He no longer looked like the fun-loving boy I had played with in the streets of Trujillo and Lisbon. "It's not—"

"What?" the captain demanded.

"It's not…kosher." David exhaled and hung his head.

Captain Caminha stepped closer to my friend. "It's…not… kosher?" With each word, he slapped David on the face. "I'll show you what's kosher!" He grimaced, as if the word left a bad taste in his mouth.

He gestured to the soldiers. "Tie him to the mast."

The soldiers did as they were told. Their eyes were hard. I knew my friend would find no pity there. Gomez ripped the shirt off David's back. All I could see were his thin shoulder blades and the knobby bones along his spine.

"Eighteen lashes," the captain ordered.

I shall never forget what passed during the next few minutes. Gomez gripped a whip with cords braided on them.

"The *gato de nueve colas*, the cat of nine tails," muttered Luis. "So cruel." His hands were balled into fists, and he turned his head away.

With each stroke of the lash, David cried out in agony. With each stroke of the lash, his voice grew fainter until, finally, it was still. I felt my heart clench in sorrow and anger, as if held in a vise. Gracia stopped her ears with her fingers and hid her face against my chest.

I put my arms around her and gazed out at the ocean. Calm. Smooth. Pitiless.

When he was done, Gomez ordered two soldiers to untie David from the mast. My friend collapsed in a bloody heap onto the deck.

Dom Mateus, the ship's doctor, knelt over David and felt for his pulse. He shook his head. "Nothing to be done. Poor boy."

Friar Escobar rushed to David's side, leaned over him, and made the sign of the cross. "Into thy hands, Lord, I commend this boy's spirit." He was about to dip his finger into a small vial of what they call their "holy oil."

David opened his eyes a slit and turned his head away. "Go... away," he croaked. I could see his lips trying to form words and faintly, ever so faintly, he whispered, "Shema Israel…" He shuddered and then lay still.

The friar backed away, as if he had heard an evil curse. Captain Caminha stared at the horizon. His wife hurried back down to her cabin. The people went back to their gossiping and idle chatter. The sailors returned to their tasks. The soldiers threw my friend's body overboard.

I grasped the mezuzah so hard that the wood dug into my skin. Silently, I mouthed the *hashkabah*, the prayer for my friend whose father had been our Rabbi Judah.

Chapter 6

Of all the horrors we faced on that floating prison—poor food, scant drinking water, filthy quarters, brutal lashings, lengthy harangues from Friar Escobar—the worst were the sharks.

Luis first told me about the sharks on the fifth day of our voyage. We had just finished what passed for breakfast—boiled beans and a cup of water—when Luis sidled up to me. I was standing next to the longboat and leaning over the rail. By then, the captain had allowed us to stay on deck for longer periods of time. He knew there was no way we could escape from the ship—except by death.

Luis pretended he was looking for something near the longboat and murmured, "Don't lean over too far or you'll be food for the sharks."

"Sharks?" In spite of the sun beating down on my head, I shuddered.

He nodded. "Lots of them in these waters." He walked over to where I was standing and spit overboard. "I hate the sight of them! I hate those small eyes—like human eyes, they are. Then there's that broad snout and razor-sharp teeth!" He shivered. "Sends a chill up and down my spine."

He pointed to a line of triangular-shaped fins poking above the water. "There they are. See them?"

I nodded and tightened my grip on the railing.

"They're following the ship, waiting for us to throw garbage... and other things...overboard."

I swallowed hard. I knew what he meant.

"They like it when we move slowly or when the ship's at a dead calm." He shook his head. "I hate them, and that's a fact."

As the days passed, the sharks had much to feast upon. A pestilence the sailors called "the bloody flux"[9] spread throughout the ship.

Almost everyone suffered with severe stomach cramps and watery diarrhea. The sick were too weak to stand, so they vomited or relieved themselves where they lay. A nauseating stench filled the hold where most of the children lay packed together. Feeble cries for water soon became silent.

I was terrified that Gracia and I would become sick, too. I did not know how the flux spread, but we tried to stay away from the people who were sick. That was nearly impossible because of the crowded conditions on the ship.

Dom Mateus could do nothing for the sick and dying. One day I heard him say to the captain, "They need more drinking water and more wholesome food."

Captain Caminha shook his head. "I can spare neither. The

journey is taking longer than I expected. There are too many mouths to feed and not enough provisions."

"But—"

The captain raised his hand. "There is nothing I can do. We are all at the mercy of the winds and the currents, the calms and the storms."

As Dom Mateus turned away, I heard him mutter, "There is always plenty to eat and drink at the captain's table."

On the seventh day after the ship left Lisbon, the midday sun blazed overhead, with only a few wispy clouds floating in a pale blue sky. The air was still; the sails scarcely moved.

A sailor had brought a child's body up from below. Gomez glanced at the body and gestured that it should be thrown overboard. Friar Escobar made the sign of the cross. He had been very busy during this voyage.

When we lived in Spain and later in Portugal, a person who died was treated with respect. The body was bathed and wrapped in a shroud. Psalms were read and the body was buried in a graveyard. This watery grave, no, this desecration, made me feel nothing but fear and loathing. And even worse, as the days passed I began to grow numb, as if a hard shell was growing around my heart.

We children were not the only ones who became ill. Many of the sailors became too weak to work. They lay on the deck or in their hammocks below deck, groaning in pain and cursing the captain and their fate.

Luis told me that many of the sailors had been tricked into debt and then given a choice—go to prison or work as a seaman on this ship. Many of them cried out that they should have chosen jail rather than this torture at sea.

We were ten days from Lisbon when Dom Mateus examined some of us older boys. "This one's healthy enough." He prodded me forward to join a small group of boys standing near the main mast. "Healthy enough to do some work."

Gomez scowled. "You'll get an extra cup of water a day and extra meat for supper. And I don't want any complaints out of you."

I remembered what had happened to my friend David. I gritted my teeth and said not a word.

He set us to work—emptying the necessary pails, washing the deck, and even working the sails and lines. In a way, I welcomed the work. Although my back ached and my hands oozed with blisters, it was still better than sitting idle on the deck with the sun beating down on my head, the endless hours stretching before me.

I enjoyed learning how the ship worked. When I was told to set the sails or climb the rigging, I could look out then and pretend I was a bird. I felt the wind rush through my body, as if I were free again. I smelled the clean salt air. Even the scrape of the rough lines in my hands made me feel I was alive.

Until then, most of the sailors had ignored us. They went about their tasks in a grinding, steady way. Only one of them kept looking at us, with an expression I could not understand. He was an African, a "negro."[10] I had seen African slaves in Lisbon, but never had I imagined one would be on this ship.

He kept to himself, eating his food alone, not taking part in the rough talk of the other sailors. He held himself erect and I liked to imagine he had once been a prince of his people, but then had been kidnapped and sold into slavery. The few words I heard him speak were Portuguese, with a musical lilt that was unique to him.

One day, the African was showing me how to weave mats made of thin rope. He was patient and did not laugh at my clumsy efforts. He looked around to make sure no one was listening. Then he put a gentle hand on my wrist. "What is your name?"

I looked into the man's deep brown eyes. "Joseph."

He furrowed his brow. "The priest told us of a Joseph in the Bible. He was taken captive and made a slave in the land of Egypt. Then you are that Joseph's namesake?"

I swallowed hard. "Yes. And no. But I do not think we are going to the land of Egypt."

"You are right." The man paused and pointed to himself. "They gave me a name. Paulo."

The way he said his name made me ask, "But you have another name?"

Paulo lowered his voice. "I do not tell my real name to one I do not know."

I understood what he meant. They called me Joseph in the world, but my Hebrew name, "Yosef," was my real name.

I nodded. "Where are you from?"

Paulo got a faraway look in his eyes. "I come from a family of fishermen on the coast. When I was a boy, I became a slave to pay

my father's debts. They ripped me from my family and my home."
He straightened his back. "I am from the Igbo tribe." He raised his
chin. "One day, I will go back to my home."

He stared at the mat we were weaving and smiled a crooked
smile. "But for now, you and I, we will do the work they tell us to
do. Yes?"

"Yes."

It was then that I had the first hint of how I might survive on
this voyage, and perhaps afterwards, to wherever we were going.
If I made myself useful, even indispensable, perhaps they would
treat me better. Right now, I was only one of many. Would I dare
to stand out from the rest? Would that be a good thing or not? My
head swirled with doubt and confusion.

While I was working, or when I lay down at night, I often
thought about Mother and Father. What had happened to them
after we were taken away? Had Father survived the blow to his
head? Had they stayed in Portugal? Or had they gone to Antwerp
as they had planned?

Wherever they were, they were probably desperate to know if
Gracia and I were still alive. Had they given in to grief or were they
still hoping we would return? Had they become Christians in the
hope that we might then be returned to them, or had they remained
Jews? My ignorance often drove me to desperate longing for the
home and family I had lost.

Most of the time, I kept my memories of Mother and Father
locked in a box in my mind, hidden away, safe. If I ever became

free, I would open the box. Until then, I would have to keep it tightly closed.

I'd had only brief glimpses of the captain's wife, Dona Maria, during the voyage. Most of the time, she stayed in her cabin. The sailors whispered that she wore only a light underdress there, due to the hot, humid weather, and that most of the time she played cards with an illuminated pack made especially for her in Spain.

But one day Dona Maria came out of her cabin, her hand in the crook of the captain's arm. She glanced at us children as if we were rats who had infested the ship. I was washing the deck and moved closer so that I could hear their conversation.

"Álvaro," Dona Maria whined, "now that my servant is ill and will probably die, who will take care of my clothes and see to my needs?"

Captain Caminha seemed lost in thought.

"Álvaro, are you listening?"

"Of course, my dear." He patted her hand. "Perhaps you can choose a girl from one of the slaves."

Dona Maria sniffed. "What do these girls know about fine clothes?"

I felt in my pocket for my mezuzah. "God give me strength," I prayed silently. I placed the mop beside the bucket and dried my hands on my pants.

I took a few steps forward and bowed. "Excuse me," I stammered. My legs were shaking so hard I could scarcely stand. The sickly sweet perfume wafting from the woman almost made me gag.

Captain Caminha scowled. "What do you want, boy? Get back to work!"

"I...I..."

"Speak up, boy!"

I swallowed hard and clutched the mezuzah more tightly. "My sister, sir—"

"What about your sister?" The captain stepped forward and raised his arm, as if to strike me.

I pointed behind me to where Gracia was sitting. "She is healthy and—"

"And what?" Dona Maria said.

"She knows how to care for clothes. Our father was a weaver. Gracia knows everything about cloth and needlework."

Dona Maria raised her eyebrows. "Really?"

"What do you want that Jewish girl for?" her husband said. "She'll eat too much and steal everything we own."

Dona Maria put her hands on her hips and turned to face him. "You persuaded me to come on this horrible voyage with you; to leave my home and my friends. The least you can do is let me have my way in this matter."

Captain Caminha shrugged. "Whatever you wish, my dear."

Dona Maria glanced at Gracia again. With a curt gesture, she said, "Bring the girl to me."

I was glad I had made Gracia wash her face and hands and comb her hair that morning. I hurried over to where she was sitting and whispered, "Hurry, Gracia. Come with me."

She glanced up and shook her head. "No. Why? Why should I?" She crossed her arms. "You're always telling me what to do. Like you're Father or something."

"The captain's wife wants to see you." I shook her arm. "Please, Gracia, hurry. Maybe you can work for her. Maybe she can help us."

Gracia slowly rose to her feet. "I hope you know what you're doing."

"I hope I do, too." I grabbed Gracia's hand and pulled her over to where Dona Maria was standing. Gracia looked at me and then at Dona Maria and made a little curtsey. She then quickly lowered her head.

"You are called Gracia?" Dona Maria asked.

Gracia nodded, but must have been too terrified to speak. For once.

Dona Maria put her finger under Gracia's chin and made her raise her head. "You are a pretty girl. I understand you are skilled at needlework."

Gracia nodded again.

"I need someone to care for my clothes and do my hair. Can you do that?"

"Yes, Dona," Gracia whispered.

"I shall give you a try then." Dona Maria wrinkled her nose. "But first, you must have a proper wash."

Gracia gazed back at me as she walked away. I could not read her expression, but it seemed to be a combination of fear, pride, and excitement.

I heard Dona Maria ask, "Can you play cards, Gracia?"

"No, Dona. But I can learn."

"Good. I shall teach you how to play piquet."

It was only then that I let out my breath.

Chapter 7
São Tomé Island
April 1493

"There it is." Luis pointed. "The island of São Tomé." He spit over the side of the ship.

"Is that where we're going?" I asked. "What's there?"

"Nothing. It's a God-forsaken island on the edge of the world." He glanced at me. "They have this idea they can grow sugarcane there. And you kids are supposed to do it." He spit again. "Stupidity and greed!"

We sailed into a natural harbor on the northeast side of the island. The first thing I noticed was the mass of trees. The jungle came so close to the shore that I felt as if I were suffocating. The air was hot and humid with the threat of a downpour.

Far to the south and west, I saw a line of black, desolate mountains rising up from the jungle. This land was as different from the places I had known—the dry hot summers of Andalusia and the cool winter of Lisbon—as night was from day.

"Be quick now!" Friar Escobar scurried among us children. "Gather your belongings and put them in your packs. We leave the ship in the morning." Beneath his flushed face, he had a sickly pallor. His hair was uncombed; his white robe was spotted with food stains and saltwater; his hands shook as he clutched his Bible to his chest.

I wondered where Gracia was and how she was doing. I had scarcely seen her since Dona Maria had chosen her, except for a brief glance now and then. We had not had a chance to talk at all. She seemed healthy enough, but I had no idea of what she was going through. *Does she still care about me?* I wondered in my selfish way. My ignorance gnawed at my belly.

The soldiers herded us onto the deck. And what a bedraggled lot we were! Dirty, half-starved, scarcely able to stand up. It had been close to three weeks since we had left Lisbon and our numbers had diminished considerably. Many children had died of the flux, but some had flung themselves overboard, so desperate were they to end their ordeal. The older ones tried to take care of the younger ones, but truth be told, scarcely a child under the age of five had survived.

All during the voyage, we children had been separated from another group of prisoners—the *degredados*, convicts from Portugal. They were a vicious lot and the captain had kept them confined below deck. For my part, I was relieved to have nothing to do with them. At night, I often heard them cursing and shouting, fighting among themselves. More than one had been tossed overboard during the voyage, having been killed in some violent argument.

Luis told me they had been given a bad choice: hang on the gallows for their crimes—forgery, robbery, murder—or go as workers to São Tomé. If they did whatever tasks they were given, however dangerous, they would gain their freedom in three years. That is, if they survived. They had chosen what they thought was the lesser of two evils.

The convicts were brought up on deck. They squinted in the bright sunlight. I could smell them from where I was standing. They were filthy and unkempt. They kept scratching under their arms and along their legs—probably from lice that were a constant ordeal to all of us.

One of them, a tall man with black eyes and olive skin, pointed at us. "What did they bring those kids here for?"

A burly man sidled up to him. He had a scar that ran along his left cheek, almost reaching his half-closed eye. His nose was crooked, as if it had been broken and never set right. "Antonio, those are the Jewish kids. The ones they kidnapped, eh?" He gazed at the island. "And brought to this armpit of the world."

"Francisco, they'll drop like flies." Antonio lowered his voice. "I heard there's all kinds of sicknesses in Africa and—"

"—and dragons and other creatures."

"They haven't got a chance." Antonio glanced at his fellow convicts and then back to the island. He grimaced. "I wonder if *we* do."

❋

The cook and Nuno, his boy, were busy gathering cooking pots and utensils, counting the clucking chickens in their cages, tugging a goat by a rope, and even herding three skinny cows into a makeshift pen.

Captain Caminha seemed to be everywhere at once—striding back and forth on the deck and barking orders. He stopped briefly, and I heard him say, "The dock is in terrible condition since João de Paiva, the last governor, was here eight years ago." That was when I realized the Portuguese had tried to settle the island before us.

I gazed at the dock with its rotting wooden planks and wondered if it would be strong enough to bear our weight, or if it would collapse and heave us all into the ocean.

A kick in the shins woke me out of my reverie. "Get out of my way!" Nuno was carrying a bulky sack on his back. Specks of what looked like pieces of onion were stuck in his matted hair. "What are you staring at?"

"Nothing. Do you…do you want some help?" I remembered how I'd helped after some of the sailors had gotten sick; how I had received extra rations. *Can I be useful here, with this Nuno? Dare I try?*

Nuno sneered and looked me up and down. "You're kind of scrawny." His mouth turned up slightly in what for him was a smile. "Like a chicken."

His breath stank. I tried not to show my disgust.

"I can do it." I held out my arms and Nuno dropped the sack into them. I staggered back with the weight of it, then took a big breath and heaved it over my shoulder. "Where do you want it?"

Nuno pointed to a corner of the deck where various sacks, boxes, and barrels had been placed. "Over there." His nose twitched, as was his habit. "And when you're done, come below deck and help me with the rest."

I began to walk away when he slapped me on the back. "Listen to what I tell you and maybe we'll get along."

For the rest of the day, I helped Nuno carry cargo onto the deck. By the time night fell, I was so tired and sore that I could scarcely stay on my feet. I plopped down under the longboat, curled up in a ball, and instantly fell asleep.

The next thing I knew, someone was shaking my shoulder and whispering, "Wake up, Joseph. Please wake up!"

I sat up so quickly that I bumped my head on the thwart of the longboat. "Ow!" I peered at Gracia in the faint light. "What is it?" I rubbed my head. "Are you all right?" I paused. "I missed you."

"I missed you, too."

I gestured for her to crawl under the boat with me. In this close-packed ship, it was the only place where we might have some privacy. When we were huddled together, she whispered in my ear, "It's a good thing you have a hard head."

I grinned. "And I see you still have a sharp tongue."

She put her finger to her lips. "Quiet!" she whispered. "I have to tell you something. But first, take this." She thrust something round and smooth into my hand.

"It's—"

"An egg. Remember?"

I hadn't eaten an egg since we had left Lisbon. "Where did you get it?"

"Dona Maria eats a hard-boiled egg every morning. There was an extra one today and I took it for you."

"But—"

"Shh. Just eat. And listen to what I have to say." She looked over her shoulder. "I can't stay long."

"What is it?" I peeled the egg and inhaled its slightly sour smell. I took a small bite. The smooth white and creamy yellow seemed to explode inside my mouth. I tried to resist gobbling up the rest of the egg, for I wanted to savor the taste to its fullest.

"I heard the captain and Dona Maria talking last night," Gracia began.

"And?"

"He was telling her about this new settlement." She paused. "He ignores me, you know. Like I'm invisible."

"Maybe that's a good thing—to sometimes be invisible."

Gracia shrugged. "They brought us here to work the land; to make sugar."

"I know. Luis told me." I nibbled a bit more of the egg.

"What do you think will happen to us?"

I drew my tongue around the inside of my mouth to get the very last bit of egg.

Gracia poked me in the shoulder. "Joseph, pay attention!"

"Sorry." I shrugged. "I don't know."

Gracia sighed. "Dona Maria says that I'll stay in their house on the island when we leave the ship tomorrow."

I nodded. "You'll be safe there."

Gracia's mouth twisted into a smile. "As safe as any of us can be. But she's got a vicious temper." She put her hand to her cheek.

"What happened?"

"Never mind. I'll be all right. What about you?"

I straightened my back and tried to look brave—whatever that looked like. "I've started helping Nuno, the cook's boy. Maybe I can work in the kitchen and not in the fields." I grinned. "Do I look like a cook to you?"

Gracia giggled. "Not much. But you'd better learn. And fast."

I clenched my fists. "I intend to. I'll show them I'm useful. I'm not a rag they can throw away when they're done with me!"

"Gracia!" Dona Maria called. "Where is that girl?"

Gracia glanced over her shoulder. "I'd better go." She kissed me on the cheek. "Be careful, Joseph."

"You too."

Chapter 8

Early the next morning, I woke up to the screaming of gulls. The air was like a heavy blanket, smothering my senses. I rubbed the sleep from my eyes and crawled out from under the longboat. I was grateful that no one had noticed me or forced me to go below deck last night.

"Line up!" barked the cook. "Hold out your bowls. Last breakfast you'll have on board the ship."

Nuno plopped a spoonful of something gray and lumpy into my bowl, along with a slice of stale bread. I tried not to stare at the bits of food in his hair.

I had scarcely finished eating when Gomez yelled, "Get your things! Line up! Time to get off the ship!"

We stared at him, not daring to believe that we were finally leaving. As terrible as the journey had been, we had settled into the routines of the ship. Now we were being thrust into an unknown world. Then I realized it wasn't only us Jewish children. This place was new to everyone.

The gentlemen in their black boots and fancy clothes stepped carefully down the gangplank. They shielded their eyes from the sun and looked back up at the ship from time to time. I heard their heavy tread on the wood, as if in time to the thumping of my heart. Did they want to turn back as I did? Well, they had a choice. I had none.

Nuno sidled up to me. "Those settlers will get the best *sesmarias*, land grants." He pointed to a short, skinny man whose movements were quick and nervous and whose head kept turning here and there, like a bird looking for a worm. "That's Dom Ortiz, the manager of the settlement."

"How do you know?"

Nuno narrowed his eyes and came closer to me. "I keep my ears open." He grinned. His teeth were yellow. "Amazing what you can hear when you serve meals to the higher-ups." He wiped his nose with the back of his hand. "They act like you're not even there, unless, of course, they want something."

I nodded. "Who are the other men?"

Nuno licked his lips and pointed with a grimy finger. "You know Dom Mateus, the doctor and apothecary."

A tall man hurried after the others, a handkerchief held to his nose, a frown pulling down his face. He had a long, full beard, brown eyes, and reddish-brown hair. "That's Dom Pereira, from Madeira. He's supposed to be an expert about growing sugarcane."

"Nuno! Come back here, you lazy, good-for-nothing boy!" the cook yelled.

"I'd better go," Nuno said. He paused and put his hand on my shoulder. "You're not a bad worker. For a Jew."

The soldiers were pushing the convicts forward and down the gangplank.

"Get your hands off me," snarled Antonio.

"Soldier scum," grumbled Francisco.

Just then, Luis grabbed my arm and pulled me aside. "I guess I won't see you again." He looked up at the tall masts, their sails now lowered. "We sailors have to stay on board—to clean the ship and make some necessary repairs." He gazed at the gray, cloud-filled sky. "Looks like rain is coming."

I breathed deeply but the air was so thick, I felt as if I were inhaling water. "Thank you. For everything." I wiped my hand on my pants and held it out to him.

Luis hesitated for a moment and then grasped my hand in his large calloused one. He put his hands on my shoulders. "You have been a good worker. Remember what I taught you."

I swallowed hard. "I will. And Luis?"

He peered around. "You'd better go. They'll be looking for you."

"But Luis, why did you help me and Gracia? Can you tell me now?"

Luis hesitated, bent down, and whispered in my ear, "I was once like you."

I grinned. "You mean, a boy?"

His mouth moved, as if he wanted to smile. "Yes. A boy. And a—"

Just then, Gomez came up to us and pushed Luis away. "What are you doing here?" he snarled. "Get back to work!"

"Yes, sir." Luis looked back at me with an expression in his eyes that I could not decipher. I wanted to know what he was going to say to me, but I never saw this kind man again.

"And you," Gomez said.

"Yes, sir?"

"Get back in line with the rest of the Jewish swine!" Gomez leaned over and spit on my shoes. "Good riddance to you!"

I was tempted to spit back at him, but the image of David's flogging filled me with dread. *Good riddance to you, too*, I thought. *And to this stinking ship!*

I shouldered my pack and scurried over to the other children. I took a deep breath and put my hand in my pocket. My heart sank. My mezuzah was gone!

I searched both my pockets and fell to my knees on the deck. The rain began to pour down in sheets, and soon I was soaked to the skin.

I ignored the rain. In my mind, I retraced my steps during the last twenty-four hours. Did my mezuzah fall out of my pocket while I was carrying the sacks for Nuno? Or while I was asleep under the longboat? Or when I stood up?

I gritted my teeth and wiped my tears with the back of my hand. They mixed with the rain until I could not tell one from the other.

There was nothing I could do. Gomez and the soldiers were pushing us off the ship—like cattle headed for branding or sheep for shearing. I followed the others down the narrow gangplank to the shore—the longest walk I had ever taken.

Chapter 9

When I first put my feet on land, everything seemed to sway, as if I were still on the ship. I didn't know if I was moving or if everyone else was or if the land was. However, I was glad to finally feel the earth under my feet.

The rain stopped suddenly and the midday sun beat down on our heads. Wisps of steam rose from the wet beach. I felt overwhelmed by all the sounds: the raucous cries of birds, the buzzing of insects, the wind through the trees.

The soldiers marched us toward a long, low wooden building smothered by vines. In one corner, a tree had taken root. It was difficult to tell what was building and what was tree.

A soldier pushed us through the narrow doorway. "Sit down over there," he ordered. The place smelled rank and moldy. We had no choice. We sat down on the filthy floor.

"My name is Corporal Lopez." He seemed to be younger than the other soldiers, for his face was unlined and he had scarcely any beard. "Don't even *think* of making trouble."

Trouble? I thought. *Why would we make trouble?* I shuddered when I remembered all the children who had died during the voyage. *How many more will die here, on this miserable island?*

A young boy and girl stood near me. They were whispering to each other and pointing at me. I pushed aside a pile of broken crockery and tried to clean a space on the dirt floor. "Here, sit down."

They looked at each other and sank down beside me.

"I didn't see you on the ship earlier," I said. "Are you—?"

"Twins?" The girl nodded and pointed to herself. "But I'm older."

"Only by fifteen minutes!" The boy peered at me. "Aren't you one of the big boys who helped sail the ship?"

Rabbi Judah had always complained that I lacked humility, but I pushed that memory aside and puffed out my chest. "My name is Joseph. What are your names?"

"I am Jacó." The boy pointed to his sister. "And that's my sister, Flor."

The two crept closer to me.

"Joseph?" Flor asked in a shaking voice.

"What?"

"Why did they bring us here?"

I shivered in spite of the oppressive heat. I knew why but I dreaded to put it into words.

"You're big," Jacó said. "You must know."

I sighed. "Sometimes I don't feel big at all. Sometimes I feel like I don't know anything." I wasn't being humble now, only truthful.

"Can we…" Flor began.

"…come closer?" Jacó finished.

I opened my arms. "Of course you can." The children's presence comforted me as, I hope, mine did them. I missed Gracia more than I expected. I had not seen her leave the ship. Dona Maria must have waited until everyone else was gone. I wondered when I would see Gracia again. I felt an ache in my heart I could not fill.

We were left alone for a long time. I must have fallen asleep, what with the strain of leaving the ship, the heat turning the building into an inferno, the buzzing of flies, and the chirping of birds. The sounds of the island blended together into one confusing cacophony.

I dreamed I was back in Trujillo. The birds were singing in the lemon tree in the courtyard of our house. Mother was humming one of her favorite songs. Lentil soup was simmering on the stove. Father's loom was clacking as he moved the shuttle back and forth. I was sitting on our old stone bench, the sun warm on my face. I was eating dates and practicing the portion of the Torah I was to read for my bar mitzvah.

"Father," I complained. "Why do I have to study this now?"

Father stopped his work. "And what else should you do, my son?"

"I want to play with David. I want to go down to the harbor and see the ships and—"

"You'll stay here and study. Stay and study. Stay and study." The sound of Father's loom got louder and louder until it filled my ears.

I woke up to the sound of pieces of wood banging against each other.

Corporal Lopez was standing in the doorway. "Get up, all of you!"

I shook Flor and Jacó. "Wake up, children!"

They rubbed their eyes, yawned, and slowly stood. I felt groggy from the heat. My throat was parched. My stomach growled for food.

"Line up facing me," Lopez ordered. "Young ones in front, older ones to the rear."

We stumbled across the uneven floor and managed to form several ragged lines.

Lopez saluted Captain Caminha as he entered the room, followed by Friar Escobar and the men who had been with us on the ship. Captain Caminha cleared his throat and frowned at a few children who were whispering. They fell silent.

"I have brought you here," he said, "on orders of good King João, to work the land; to grow and produce sugar." He waved a buzzing fly away from his face. "This island is a good one. The soil is fertile; the climate is hot and humid; there is plenty of water from the rivers and an abundance of timber."

He gestured to the men who were standing behind him. "These men have come to settle this island. Each has received a land grant from the king. Each will choose several of you to work for him. In return, you will receive food, clothing, and shelter—enough for your needs.

The captain glanced at Friar Escobar, who cleared his throat and said, "Every Sunday, you will attend Mass in the chapel near this building."

The captain narrowed his eyes. "Anyone who misses Mass or one of the lessons in the Christian faith will be punished."

I put my hand in my pocket, but felt only the rough material against my fingers. I wished I could hide behind a rock, a tree, a bush—anywhere but from this man's piercing stare.

He pointed at several of the boys who looked bigger and stronger than me. "You. You. And you. Come with me." He paused. "I'll take three of you girls, too." He spoke to the men standing behind him. "Now, choose whom you wish." He snapped his fingers. "My slaves, follow me." With these words, he strode away, as if we no longer existed.

The men walked along the rows. I tried to watch them under lowered lids. *Who would show kindness? Who would be cruel?* I felt as if I were in a twisted version of a game where the leaders choose who will be on their teams. The best players are chosen first; the worst players, last. But this was no game.

Dom Pereira, the master of sugar, stood in front of me. He put his finger under my chin and jerked my head up. "Look at me, boy."

I gazed into his hard eyes.

"Can you read and write?" He smirked at the other men. "Most of these Jews (the word sounded dirty when he said it) can read." He shrugged. "Maybe they think that with their learning they can trick us out of our wealth." He turned back to me. "Boy, I asked

64

you a question!" He gripped my arm in a hard vise. "Answer now, and be quick about it!"

"Yes…Yes, sir. I can read and write Spanish, Portuguese, and… Hebrew."

Dom Pereira smiled, but it was not a real smile. "You may prove useful eventually. I will take you."

I was chosen, along with four other boys and two girls. I was glad that Flor and Jacó were among them.

Dom Pereira waved his hand. "Get your things. Follow me."

It was then, only then, that I realized I was a slave. Completely and utterly. Dom Pereira *owned* me. He could do anything he wanted with me. I was his property and worth only as much as my labor would profit him.

I gritted my teeth and resolved that I would do what this man ordered. At the same time, I would learn as much as I could. I would make myself useful here on this miserable island. I was a human being, a person of worth, no matter how Dom Pereira treated me. I would survive.

Chapter 10

Each settler, including the convicts, was assigned a house—the size according to his importance in the community. Captain Caminha had the largest house. It was one-story, made of rough stone, with wooden shingles and waxed paper covering the holes for windows.

Dom Pereira had the next largest house, also made of stone. His knowledge and skill were supposed to make a profit for the settlers and, of course, for the king. I was surprised to see that his house was no bigger than the one my family had owned in Trujillo.

We slaves lived in a wooden hut behind the master's house. I slept on the floor on a rough pallet filled with dry leaves. I ate wherever I could—usually squatting outside the hut if it wasn't raining. The latrine, where we relieved ourselves, was behind the hut. I used the huge green leaves from plants growing beside the path to wipe myself. When the wind blew toward the hut, the stink of human waste was nauseating.

At night, tiny insects crept out of my pallet. Even though I tried to wrap myself in the thin blanket Dom Pereira had given me, each morning I was covered with red bites so that I scratched my skin raw with the itching.

Every day except Sunday, we were marched to the tract of land each settler had been given. We hacked at weeds and tangled undergrowth with machetes; we chopped down trees with axes.

My arms and face burned and flaked. On the ship, my hands had blistered. Now, it seemed, there were new places that had not blistered before. I longed for the soothing salves that Mother had applied whenever I had skinned a knee or bruised an elbow. I longed for her tender caresses and calming words. Here, there was no one and nothing that could comfort me.

In drenching rain and oppressive heat, I helped clear one patch of ground after another. I dropped into an exhausted sleep at the end of each day. While I was sleeping, it seemed that the forest grew back over the ground we had just cleared.

One day, I heard Dom Ortiz ask my master, "Why can't they burn the bush instead of clearing it by hand? They make no progress like this."

Dom Pereira's face turned red and he yelled, "Are you mad? Do you not know what happened in Madeira when the settlers set fire to the bush?"

"No, but—"

"The fire burned out of control, destroying everything we had built or planted. We had to seek safety in the sea, staying up to our necks for two days so we wouldn't be burned alive!"

Captain Caminha tried to keep his promise that we would receive food, shelter, and clothing. But soon the provisions of flour, cheese, and olive oil that had been brought from Portugal began to run low. I felt a constant gnawing hunger. My shirt and pants were in tatters from the sun and rain, and from the grueling work in the fields. But I was too tired to care. All I could think of was putting food in my belly and doing the minimum amount of work necessary to escape a flogging.

Even worse than the hunger was the loneliness. The Sunday after Mass a week or two after our arrival, Gracia stopped me as I was leaving the chapel and whispered, "Dona Maria said I can't see you anymore." She gripped my arm tightly. "She doesn't want me mixing with the rest of the slaves. She says…she says that you're not really Christians and that you'll corrupt me."

Gracia glanced over her shoulder and gave me a quick hug. "Take care of yourself, Joseph. You're the only family I have left." I saw tears in her eyes as she hurried away. My throat was tight as I gazed at her retreating back.

I knew I would be whipped if I went to Captain Caminha's house. I could not send Gracia a note. She had never learned to read. My sister was close, but so very far away.

Several weeks later, work slackened and then came to a dead halt. But not for a good reason. Almost everyone became ill with a sickness the doctor called "tertian fever."[11] Every morning, our numbers were smaller.

Dom Mateus tried to cure the sick, but his remedies such as bleeding or leeches were useless. Then he himself contracted the illness. He suffered uncontrollable chills, shaking, and a high fever. He seemed to get better for a few days, but then he was struck again. He was dead within two weeks of the outbreak.

After that, the settlement had no physician, except for the convict Antonio. He had been a barber back in Portugal. But few people wanted him to get too close to them. It was rumored that he had murdered a man while in a frenzy of jealousy over a woman.

One morning shortly after the doctor died, I woke up sweating so much that my clothes and pallet were soaked. After that, I do not remember much. I was swallowed up in dreams. I could not tell what was real and what was not.

Once, I felt a cooling cloth on my brow and saw Gracia kneeling beside me. I thought I heard her say, "Please, Joseph! Get better! Don't leave me!"

In my delirium, I thought I saw Mother and Father holding hands and floating in the air above me. And then it was Dom Pereira standing over my pallet, shaking his head and muttering, "He was a good worker. It will be a shame to lose him."

I woke up with a thirst such as I had never felt before. The little girl, Flor, was sitting beside my pallet and offered me a cup of water. I drained it down and gestured for another. After the third cup, I managed to croak, "How long have I been ill?"

Flor wrung out a cloth and placed it on my forehead. "Five days. But you're better now."

I nodded weakly. "It seems that I am."

"Jacó and I were worried about you." She hung her head. "You're the only person who's been kind to us."

I reached out and grasped her small hand in mine. "I'll be fine now." I managed a smile. "Thank you for taking care of me."

Flor gazed at me with her dark eyes. "I wasn't the only one." She looked back over her shoulder. "A big girl came from the captain's house. She said she's your sister."

I tried to sit up, but flopped down again. "Gracia?"

Flor nodded. "Yes. That's her."

I exhaled slowly. "Thank God she's still all right."

I closed my eyes then and sank back into sleep. When I awoke, long shadows filled the hut. A bowl of soup and a cup of water were on the floor beside me. I rolled onto my side and gulped the soup down. Over the next few days, the fever lessened and my shaking subsided.

When Dom Pereira strode into the hut and stood over my pallet, he sniffed and grimaced—probably from the foul air in the hut. "I see that you are finally back with the living!" He paced back and forth. "You will not be fit to work in the fields for a long time. When you recover fully, you will work as my assistant. I need someone who can read and write, as well as do basic arithmetic."

"Yes, master."

"Good. Come see me when you feel stronger." With those words, he strode out of the hut.

Three days later, I managed to walk to Dom Pereira's house to begin my new work. I was grateful that I no longer had to labor in the fields. I had learned some skills on the ship. Now I hoped to learn something about sugar. *I will be useful*, I thought. *I* will *be useful!*

The world seemed brighter then; the air cleaner. I breathed deeply, as if I had been given a new chance for life. But chances were few and far between on the island of São Tomé.

One day shortly after I began working for Dom Pereira, Jacó was clearing the bush and stepped on a black cobra. The cobra reared its head and sank its fangs into the boy. Jacó fell down and could not move. Within the hour, he was dead.

Dom Pereira ordered two of us older boys to take Jacó's body to the graveyard and the rest of the slaves to continue working. We recited the hashkabah before we returned to work. Neither of us could remember all the words, but we said what we could. We were glad that Friar Escobar arrived late for the burial. We would have been punished for saying our Jewish prayer for the dead.

After Jacó's death, Flor went about her tasks with a dullness I hadn't seen before. I tried to talk to her, but she answered in only one or two words. She would stare into space, her eyes empty and unseeing. At night, she curled up in a tight ball on her pallet. She would cry out from bad dreams. Then she would crawl over to me and lay her thin body next to mine. I would wrap my arms about her. She seemed so frail then—as if she were more spirit than flesh.

One Sunday a few weeks after Jacó's death, Flor went down to the river to wash her clothes.

"She was gone in an instant," one of the young boys told me later. "In an instant."

"But how? Where?"

The boy's shoulders shook and his voice trembled. "We were all down by the river. A crocodile swam up to shore, close, close." He closed his eyes, trying to remember, trying to forget. "Then, *snap*." He opened his eyes. The tears ran down his face. "Flor was gone."

I collapsed to the floor. I put my head on my knees and wrapped my arms around my legs. I wept until I had no more tears left. *How many more people will die?* I wondered. *Will we ever be free?*

Friar Escobar was busy, saying funeral masses and burying the dead in the ever-expanding graveyard. When he wasn't doing that, he forced us to listen to endless harangues about his Savior; about the Devil and temptation; about heaven and hell. While the friar talked, I pretended he was only an angry mosquito who might sting me, but was of no real importance.

I kept wondering how the sprinkling of his holy water could change who I was or how I had been raised. I often longed for my mezuzah.

And yet, some of the Jewish slaves—especially the younger ones—responded to the friar's words with enthusiasm. They seemed to drink in his teachings and slowly forget their Jewish identity.

One Sunday, I saw Gracia kneeling down in the chapel, clutching a tiny cross that Dona Maria must have given her, and mouthing the Christian prayers. I wanted to yank the cross from her neck and throw it into the river or, even better, into the ocean. I had to fight to keep myself in check.

I tried to talk to her after the service, but she turned her face away and hurried off behind Dona Maria. I was left with a sick feeling in the pit of my stomach. I was losing Gracia. Like water through my fingers, she was slipping away, slipping away.

Chapter 11

"I must have more workers," Dom Pereira said. "We have already been here three months, and I cannot begin sugar production with only these useless Jewish children."

I was standing behind Dom Pereira, who had come to speak to Captain Caminha.

"I have sent the ship to El Mina, our fortress on the coast," the captain said. "Gomez will buy African slaves there; slaves who know how to work the land."

"In Madeira, most of our workers were families or hired workers. We had only a few slaves."

The captain frowned. "What you did on Madeira will not work here."

"But—"

Captain Caminha pounded his fist on the table. "It will not work, I say! Here, we must produce sugar on a large scale to make it profitable. And for that, we must use—"

Dom Pereira lowered his voice. "Slaves."

"We did not have to buy the Jewish slaves, but the Africans will not come so cheaply."

Dom Pereira sighed. "And what will we live on in the meantime? Until the sugarcane is grown, harvested, processed, and sent back to Portugal? Until a ship comes here with provisions? Are we to live on air?"

Captain Caminha put his hand on Dom Pereira's arm. "Duarte, I beg you. Do not despair. Have patience. We shall make São Tomé a profitable settlement."

"But how?" Dom Pereira looked defeated.

"While we wait, each man will have a large garden plot. We will grow crops that are suitable to this climate."

"What do you suggest?"

"I have heard that yams, millet, beans, and bananas grow well here. Oil we will get from the palm trees." The captain paused. "I have also heard of a new plant called maize. We might try to grow it here."

Dom Pereira sighed again. "How I miss the good oil from home! And freshly baked bread!"

"We must all make sacrifices," the captain said.

Does he care about the sacrifices he has forced us Jews to make? I wondered.

A few days later, Gomez returned from El Mina. We all hurried down to the shore, for we were eager to see what the ship had brought back. We were hoping for provisions of meat, rice, flour, and even my favorite—beans.

The upper class of the settlement, including the captain and my master, stood in front, the convicts behind them, and we Jewish children at the very back. For us slaves, it was a welcome change from our unceasing toil.

As the ship approached, I heard the sound of human cries and of something being thrown into the water.

Dom Pereira called to me, "Here, boy. Come closer." I hurried to his side. I was hesitant to speak, but I was curious. "What are they throwing into the water, master?"

Dom Pereira glanced at me and then back at the ship. "Africans, boy."

"People? They're throwing *people* into the water?" I swallowed hard. I remembered the hungry sharks that had followed the ship during our long voyage to the island.

He nodded. "They used to do the same thing in Madeira." His gaze never left the ship. "If they're dead, they are thrown overboard. If they're sick, they are thrown overboard."

"But—"

Dom Pereira made an impatient gesture. "Do you want to get sick with whatever pestilence they bring?"

"No, but—"

"Enough of your foolish questions!"

I backed away, feeling sick to my stomach. I bent over and vomited in the sand. I tasted sourness in my mouth and, out of habit, put my hand into my empty pocket.

The ship entered the bay and dropped anchor alongside the dock. The gangway was lowered and Friar Escobar hurried onto the ship. He was eager to sprinkle his holy water on the Africans; to read his Bible to them in a language they did not understand.

As Gomez and the soldiers pushed the slaves down the gangway, Dom Ortiz counted each one. With every number, his black eyebrows came together in one line. He reminded me of a fat beetle. "One, two, three…"

Then I heard a sound I shall never forget—the clanking of chains. Thick iron rings connected by heavy links of chain encased the men's necks, wrists, and ankles. We Jewish children were slaves, but at least we had not been bound by chains.

"Four, five, six…"

The Africans stared in terror at the men guarding them. Their backs were bent low. These Africans were nearly naked, except for a scrap of cotton around their private parts.

The soldiers lined the beach up to the settlement. They had swords and armor, guns and cannons. What could the Africans do against such firepower?

"Seven, eight, nine, ten…"

Then came the women, a few with babies clutched to their chests. Several young children walked beside the women, who looked with terror at the soldiers and at the rest of us who had crowded onto the beach. At least, these women were not bound by chains. A small blessing.

"Eleven, twelve, thirteen, fourteen…"

I wanted to put my hands over my ears and shut out the sounds, but I knew that Dom Pereira would slap my face, or worse, if I tried.

"Ortiz!" Captain Caminha said.

"Yes, captain?"

"Are you finished counting?"

"Yes, captain."

"Take the slaves to the building where we first put the Jews. Give them water, feed them, but do not remove their chains."

"Yes, captain."

"Tomorrow, I will distribute these slaves to our settlers."

Ortiz carried a whip in his hand and cracked it close to the feet of the Africans standing at the front of the line. They jumped, startled, and several began to moan. "Move!" he shouted.

They gazed at Ortiz, not understanding his words.

"Bring the slave, Paulo," the captain ordered.

Paulo hurried down the gangway and spoke to the Africans in his language. He pointed toward the settlement, and made a gesture of eating and drinking. The Africans seemed to understand and began to plod away.

Paulo sighed and slowly made his way back to the ship. I never saw Paulo again. I often wondered what happened to him; whether he was taken ill and died, or whether he finally gained his freedom.

The Africans shuffled up the beach. One boy looked at me as he passed. The look was brief, like the flicker of a candle. I took a step toward the boy.

Friar Escobar was hurrying behind the Africans and hissed, "You

Anne Dublin

stay away from them!" He elbowed past me. "I will show them the true path to salvation!"

My heart broke for these Africans. They did not know what they would be facing, but I knew all too well.

After the Africans arrived, things changed in the settlement. The men used machetes to clear the land and hoes to prepare the soil. The women, more numerous than the men, were put to work at other tasks: planting and weeding, as well as domestic chores such as cooking, cleaning, and washing clothes.

Dom Pereira obtained three women, one with a baby at her breast, two men, and the boy who had stared at me when he arrived on the island.

Gomez had also brought a few African cows and a bull, and even some goats and chickens. Now we had an occasional cup of milk along with our daily meal of beans.

Life in the settlement staggered on.

Several fields were cleared and Dom Pereira showed the workers how to plant the canes. With their hoes, they had to clear a plot of land five feet square and five inches deep. In the middle of each square, the women planted sugar cane buds that Dom Pereira had brought from Madeira. They covered these buds with soil.

If the cane took root, the weeders spent all day picking away the undergrowth that could choke the cane stalks. They had to ignore the rats that scuttled over their feet and the bladelike cane leaves that slashed their wrists and arms. The rats must have come off the ship when we landed, for I heard Ortiz say there had been no rats on the island before we arrived.

Ten months later, Dom Pereira became ill with the tertian fever. With every passing day, he grew worse. After just a week, his body had wasted away and his skin was thin as parchment. Before the sugar stems began to flower, Dom Pereira was dead.

Chapter 12
Spring 1494

I did not grieve for Dom Pereira. How could I? He had chosen to come to São Tomé in order to make his fortune. He had worked us until he was satisfied that the island could grow sugar cane. He had not been cruel; he had not been kind. He had treated us as if we were field animals. Nothing more. Nothing less.

On the evening after his funeral, we were sitting around our fires outside the huts—the Jewish slaves around one, the Africans around another. I heard the buzzing of insects, the call of birds, the distant crash of waves upon the rocks.

"What will happen to us now that our master is dead?" asked Ephraim, another slave boy. I shook my head. "I don't know. Maybe things will get better." I shuddered. "Maybe they'll get worse."

The dark sky was filled with a mass of stars so bright that I felt I could reach out and touch each one and put it in the palm of my hand. When I was young in Trujillo, Father and I used to stand at night in the courtyard of our house. He would point at the constellations of the stars. On this island off the coast of Africa, so far from home, I gazed at the star cluster called Aquarius.

Father had told me that in the Greek myth, Aquarius was a handsome young boy called Ganymede. Zeus, the king of the gods, decided to kidnap the boy and sent an eagle to snatch Ganymede out of the fields where he was watching over his sheep. Father had paused before saying, "Ganymede became the cupbearer for the gods on Mount Olympus."

At the time, it was only a story to me. But now I felt like that young boy who had been taken from everything he had loved and deposited into an alien land. I felt such anger then, such sorrow, but I did not know what to do with it.

One of the African men was beating on an empty gourd with a stick; another was blowing on a kind of flute made from a hollowed-out reed; a third was shaking a container filled with something that rattled—probably dried beans or pebbles. As they played, the women chanted softly—a song filled with sadness and longing.

When there was a pause, I began to hum the lullaby Mother used to sing to Gracia and me.

Nani, nani,
Nani kere el ijo,
El ijo de la madre,
De chiko se aga grande.

The baby wants a lullaby,
Mother's little boy—
He will grow up tall.[12]

The Jewish children sang with me; the Africans gradually joined in, accompanying us with their instruments.

Suddenly, I felt a tap on my shoulder. "You are Joseph?" the African boy said.

I nodded. "How do you know my name?"

The boy sat down beside me. He picked up a stick and began to peel its bark with his fingernails. "I heard…the master talk to you." His words came out slowly, hesitantly. I was surprised that he spoke Portuguese at all after such a short time.

"What is your name?" I said.

The boy glanced at me and then quickly looked down. "They call me Tomás. But that is not my real name." He hesitated. "A real name has…what you say?…power. It is only for family and… friends."

I nodded. "My people also have one name for the family and a different name for outside the home."

Tomás was quiet as he peeled the stick with nimble fingers. The light from the fire made his skin glow. When he looked up again, I could see flickers of gold in his dark brown eyes.

"Your people? But you are…a slave," Tomás said.

I nodded. "Like you."

Tomás shook his head. "No. Not like me." He pointed at my

skin. "You are white. You speak…" he gestured vaguely into the air, "what they speak. You read…from books."

"But I am a slave, too."

"You are a slave, but not like me!" He rose abruptly, threw the stick far into the bushes, and hurried back to the other Africans.

I wrapped my arms around my knees and stared at the fire. *How could I have been so stupid?*

Early the next morning, I was awakened by a shouted command. "Get up, all of you! Move your backsides!"

Dom Ortiz stood at the door of the hut. I could not see his face, for the light was behind him. I imagined his beetle brows joined together and his mouth pressed into a single thin line. He held a grayish piece of cloth to his nose.

Beside him was Corporal Lopez, the soldier who had stood guard over us when we had first come to the island. I tried to catch his eye, but he ignored me. "Stand up and pay attention!" Lopez barked.

I rose groggily to my feet along with the others.

"Captain Caminha has given you to me," Dom Ortiz began. "You are my slaves now. You will follow my orders." He paused and mopped his forehead with his handkerchief. "I am determined to make this colony work." He stared at each of us. "Dom Pereira was too soft on you. From now on, you will work as you've never worked before."

He gestured for me to come closer. "You! Boy!"

I edged toward him, my heart pounding.

"Yes?" I said.

"Yes, *what*?"

I licked my dry lips. "Yes, master."

"I hear you're one of those clever Jews." Dom Ortiz scowled. "Maybe too smart for your own good."

I shrugged.

Dom Ortiz slapped my face so hard that my ears rang. Then he grabbed me by the hair. "You will answer when I speak to you." With every syllable, he yanked my hair again. "Do. You. Un-Der-Stand?" My scalp felt like it was on fire.

"Yes, master," I gasped.

"Good." He let go of my hair, stepped back, and wiped his hands on his pants. "Now, come with me."

As I left the hut, I heard one boy say, "Why is he so special?"

"He always thinks he's smarter than the rest of us," said another.

"Leave him alone," Ephraim said. "There's nothing he can do about it anyway."

"You're right," said the first boy. "He's a slave, just like the rest of us."

"He'd better be careful," said the second boy. "Around here, it's better not to be noticed."

I followed my new master out of the hut and into what had been Dom Pereira's house. Everything was as he had left it, for Dom Pereira had been an orderly man. The table and benches were in their usual place; books and papers were stacked neatly on a small shelf. The house now belonged to Dom Ortiz—just as we slaves belonged to him.

Dom Ortiz sat down on the chair at the end of the table. He stared into the air for a long minute, tapping his fingers together. Then he glanced up at me.

"Your name?"

"Joseph…Belifonte."

Dom Ortiz sneered. "A good *Jewish* name." He rubbed his hands together. "Dom Pereira taught you how to make sugar?"

"He…he was starting to, but—"

"What?"

"He got sick before I learned much."

"Then…you do not know exactly how?"

I shivered in spite of the oppressive heat inside the house. How should I answer this man? I had the feeling that, no matter what I said, it would be wrong. "I…I don't know how to make sugar, but I can learn."

Ortiz jumped to his feet and pounded his fist on the table. "You will learn, boy, or you will go back to the fields!"

He gestured toward the books. "Perhaps they will help." He paused. "I will give you one week. I must speak with the captain now."

With these words, he strode out of the house. As he left, I heard him mutter, "Books! They were never much good to me."

My legs shook so hard I could scarcely move, but I walked toward the books and took one off the shelf. I sat down and began to read. The words blurred before my eyes.

Chapter 13

I tried. I really tried. Dom Pereira had left one or two slim volumes about growing and processing sugar. They described the methods used in the Azores and in Madeira. Before he died, he had explained to me that the climate and soil were different here on São Tomé. Then I had a sickening thought: What would happen to me, to us, if we *couldn't* make the sugar?

Every evening, Dom Ortiz walked over to the fire where I sat with the other slaves. Every evening, he asked the same question, "Well, boy, what have you learned today?"

And every evening, I murmured, "A little more, master. A little more."

He would swear under his breath and stalk away.

I could find little information and, as the days passed, I began to imagine the various punishments that Dom Ortiz would inflict upon me. The more frightened I became, the less I was able to grasp any information. I often woke up in the middle of the night and was not able to go back to sleep.

But then I had a stroke of good luck.

I had read everything I could find among Dom Pereira's books and papers. Dom Ortiz had ordered me to stay in the sitting room, but one day while he was gone, I looked into the bedroom. Perhaps I was bored or angry or simply curious. Who knows why I disobeyed Dom Ortiz?

Dom Pereira's bed was a wooden frame with a thin mattress on top of heavy crisscrossed ropes attached to the frame. On the bed was a woolen blanket and a pillow.

I glanced over my shoulder, crept to the bed, and felt the mattress and pillow for lumps. Nothing. A large black spider scurried out from under the bed. I shuddered and crossed my arms. I have always been terrified of spiders.

I took a big breath, wiped my forehead with the back of my hand, and peeked under the bed. I wanted to be sure there were no more spiders lurking there. A book covered in brown leather lay in the thick dust.

I picked it up and started to riffle through the pages. It was Dom Pereira's journal—written from the year 1485 until close to the time of his death. I clutched the book to my chest, stood up, and walked back to the sitting room.

I began to read the journal. As I did, I imagined Dom Pereira's long, full beard, his brown eyes, his reddish-brown hair. I remembered his ink-stained fingers and his yellow fingernails. I remembered his cursing when his cuff got smeared with ink. I almost missed the man; compared to Dom Ortiz, he had treated me fairly.

I read that journal as if my very life depended on it. And perhaps it did. Here I learned details about sugarcane—how to grow, harvest, and process it into sugar. I sighed with relief as I read the words. I read until the light faded. Dom Ortiz had not given me permission to light a candle, so I made my way to where the slaves were sitting outside near the fires.

My stomach was growling with hunger; my eyes were sore. But I felt a huge load had been lifted from my shoulders as I plopped onto the ground and held my hands out to the flickering flames. I could not keep my eyes open.

"Joseph?" Tomás said. "Are you...all right?" Since our argument, Tomás and I had gradually grown closer. Perhaps, as they say, misery loves company. Perhaps, he came to understand that we were all slaves together—black and white. I do not know his reasons, but I was grateful for his friendship.

I jerked my head up. "Yes. Just tired." My stomach rumbled and I grinned. "And very hungry. I think I could eat a horse."

Tomás looked at me quizzically. "A horse? What is that?"

"It's an animal with four legs, a strong back, and a swishing tail."

Tomás still looked puzzled.

"Look. I'll draw it for you." I picked up a stick and drew a rough picture of a horse in the sand.

"That looks like...a sick hippopotamus."

"What's a hippopotamus?"

Tomás smiled. "It is like a fat horse. But it swims in the water."

I smiled back at him. My stomach growled again.

"Wait." Tomás held up his hand. "I will bring you food." He rose and walked over to an African woman who was stirring the contents of a pot. He spoke a few words to her, pointed to me, and then to the pot. She nodded and ladled something hot into a wooden bowl.

Tomás held the bowl with both hands as he walked back to where I was sitting. He squatted down and handed the bowl to me. "Eat."

I glanced at him and said, "*Obrigado*. Thank you." I inhaled the delicious aroma of the soup and blew on it.

"The woman over there is a good cook," Tomás said.

"What is in it?"

Tomás counted on his fingers. "Beans. Fish. Vegetables from the garden."

"The garden?"

"Yes. The women have planted a small garden."

"That's wonderful!"

I sipped the soup slowly. In a strange way, it reminded me of Mother's soup. Some of the ingredients were different, but this woman had the skill, like Mother, to make tasty food from very little.

I picked up chunks of fish and vegetables at the bottom of the bowl with my fingers, licked the bowl clean, and sighed. I set the bowl on the ground and stared into the fire.

"Joseph?" Tomás was scratching a design in the sand.

"Yes?"

"Will you...will you teach me...the letters?" He paused and looked at me with an expression I could not understand.

"You want me to teach you how to read?"

Tomás nodded and looked over his shoulder.

"But…Africans aren't allowed to learn to read." Now it was my turn to look behind me. I swallowed hard. "We could get whipped… or worse."

Tomás continued to trace patterns on the ground.

I remembered how he had gazed at me when he arrived on the island; how the Africans had allowed me to join them at their fire; how he had often brought food for me.

"Why do you want to learn to read?" I asked.

Tomás gazed into the distance. "Back home…I had no need to read." He straightened his back. "I was learning to be a hunter, like my father and his father before him. But I was taken by slave traders who came into my village." He lowered his voice and looked at me sideways. "I will not always be a slave."

He paused, took a big breath, and let it out slowly. "When I go from this place, I must know their language. Back home, I had a spear and bow and arrows for my weapons. Here, the reading will be my weapon."

His words touched me. "I will help you." I gritted my teeth. "Whatever the cost."

Tomás clapped his hands. "When will we start?"

I smiled and put my hand on Tomás's arm. "Now is a good time."

Chapter 14

I did not have a lot of time to give Tomás reading lessons. The next weeks were exhausting for all of us. The sugarcane had grown higher than my head. Dom Ortiz pushed us to harvest it and process the sugar.

First, he ordered the strongest African men to go to the mountains to search for a suitable stone to use as a grindstone. Luckily, the convict Francisco had been a stonemason back in Portugal—until he had "accidentally" dropped an immense block of stone on top of a man who had been blackmailing him. I never found out for what.

Francisco had brought his stone-cutting tools—chisels, wedges, and such like—and seemed to walk straighter now that he had been given a task at which he was skilled.

The evening before the workers were supposed to leave for the mountains, Francisco came to the house to speak to Dom Ortiz. I stood against the wall and hoped they wouldn't notice me.

"Do you have everything you will need to cut the stone and bring it back?" Dom Ortiz asked.

Francisco sat down heavily on the bench and scowled. "I know my trade. I have everything." He was drinking a cup of some of the precious wine that had been brought from Portugal.

"And enough workers?"

Francisco shrugged. "Enough. But these Africans are lazy." He sipped the wine and wiped his mouth with the back of his hand. "It is hard to get work out of them."

"They *must* do it!" Dom Ortiz punched his fist into his open hand. "Without the stone, we cannot crush the cane." He narrowed his eyes. "And without the sugar, we cannot make a profit."

Francisco spread his thick fingers on the table. "Look, Ortiz. I can only do what I can do. You should not expect the impossible."

Dom Ortiz glared at Francisco. "Unfortunately, in this cursed place, the impossible is what we must do." He scowled. "If you need to, use the whip."

Francisco nodded. "No problem there. But I want to know how you'll turn the wheel."

Dom Ortiz glanced at me. "Here we have slaves. They will turn the stone." His eyebrows came together. "They will turn the stone. Or they will taste the whip."

Five days later, Francisco came back to the settlement. He had set out with eight Africans. Only seven returned. The eighth man had slipped and fallen off a cliff. I wondered if he had jumped. He would not have been the first.

The men were covered with cuts, bruises, and insect bites. They dragged a heavy stone using thick ropes, and—grunting—pushed it into the pit that other slaves had dug while they were away.

While they worked, I kept thinking of the words in the Passover *Haggadah*: "And the Egyptians did evil unto us and tormented us and set upon us hard labor."[13] Deep in my bones, I felt a connection with the misery of those Israelite slaves in ancient times and our misery now.

Francisco showed the slaves how to install the driveshaft. In three days, and after much cursing—Friar Escobar plugged his ears in passing—the grinding stone was ready.

Dom Ortiz had kept us busy during the time the men were away. He forced us to construct the "sugar house" and to cut huge stacks of firewood. Finally, he had ordered us to haul out the copper pots, pans, and utensils that Dom Pereira had guarded so carefully.

All was ready: grindstone, driveshaft, pots, firewood. Then our labor truly began.

Day after day, some of the men and women cut the thick cane stalks. They loaded the heavy canes into carts; others pulled the carts to the pit and dumped the cane there. More slaves turned the driveshaft for hours at a time. After the canes were crushed, they carried the cane juice to the sugar house.

I was not exempt from the labor. In the sugar house, the women and we older children skimmed off the impurities that rose to the surface as the juice was boiled in the huge pots over a constant fire. The juice was boiled again and again—each time in smaller pots.

The sugar house was like the inferno of hell that Friar Escobar spoke about so often during his endless Sunday sermons. We were all dirty, sweaty, blackened by smoke. We were all scorched by the fire or by the hot sugar. We all had burns on our hands, arms, even chests and legs. But we could not stop to tend to our wounds. We had to keep going, going, going.

Time after time, Dom Ortiz asked me, "Is it pure enough yet?"

"I cannot tell. I've never done this before." The words choked in my throat. "I can only guess from what Dom Pereira wrote."

"If it is not good enough, you will pay for it!"

We worked late into the night. We were often too tired to eat, but collapsed onto our pallets until the early morning light crept into our huts. Then the whole torturous process began all over again. I often wished this island had fewer trees, so that we would run out of firewood and the fires would at last go out.

Finally, when I thought the syrup was clear enough, I told the workers to pour it into inverted earthenware cones. It dripped through a hole in the tip of the cone, cooled, and eventually a loaf of golden-brown sugar was formed that was dry and pure.

At that time, I could scarcely think from one day of toil to another. When the sugar was finally made and we had a few days to rest, I began to think about our situation. I wondered why we tolerated such horrible work and abuse.

We had few options. Where could we go if we escaped? Inland to the mountains? Perhaps. But what would we eat? How would we survive? And what would happen if we were found and brought back to the settlement?

Could we rebel against our masters with their swords and their guns? Even if we overcame them, where would we go? No one knew how to sail a ship. We would be stranded on this cursed island forever.

We would never be granted our freedom. We were too valuable. These Portuguese needed us in order to make a profit. They would keep us alive—just alive enough to get the maximum work out of us and for Friar Escobar to save our souls.

Most of us decided to do the best we could; to cling to life; to survive. There was no other choice.

Chapter 15

The Sunday after the sugar was finished, while the other slaves were leaving the chapel after Mass, Friar Escobar blocked my way. He smelled of sweat and unwashed clothes as he put a heavy hand on my shoulder. "Wait," he said. "You are the boy called Joseph?"

I nodded.

"I need to speak to you."

He gestured for me to follow him. I did not need to crane my neck to look up at him, for I was almost his height now. For the past few months, my voice had been changing; hair was growing on my chest and under my arms. *If I ever see Mother and Father again, will they recognize me?* I wondered.

The friar sat down heavily on a bench outside the low, rough building. He picked up a large leaf from the ground and fanned his face.

He squinted at me. "How old are you?"

I squirmed. "Why do you want to know?"

Friar Escobar scowled. "Just tell me."

"What month is it?"

"It is May, in the year of our Lord 1494."

"Then I am fourteen years old." I swallowed hard. "My birthday was in April." My throat tightened. I had been enslaved for more than one year.

Friar Escobar stroked his stubbly chin. "Fourteen already. Then you must prepare for your first confession."

I wanted to shout, "I won't! I don't *want* to!" But I suppressed the urge. "I...I don't know how to do that."

"Do not worry, my son. I will teach you the words."

As I sat there sweating in the morning sun, I learned to recite the Latin words. I felt like a *papagaio*, a parrot squawking high up in the trees.

"Bless me, Father, for I have...sinned," I said. "For these and any sins I may have forgotten, I am truly...sorry." *What did I have to be sorry about?*

Friar Escobar put the leaf down on his lap and crossed himself. "I absolve you from your sins in the name of the Father, the Son, and the Holy Spirit." He stared at me. "Now make the sign of the cross."

What choice did I have? If I didn't do as he said, he would have me whipped. I had seen him do it to others. He would not hesitate to do it to me.

I gritted my teeth and crossed myself.

"Go in peace, my son."

I sprang up and walked away as quickly as I could. I was seething inside. *I will not have peace until I am free. These Portuguese kidnapped us from our homes and families. These Portuguese brought us to this foul island of disease and death. These Portuguese are the ones who should confess. Not me.* I balled my hands into fists. *And if there is a God, their confessions would make Him weep.*

The next evening, we were all sitting around the fire after we finished our meal. The storyteller was the same woman who had cooked the good soup Tomás had brought me. He plopped down by my side.

I pointed to the woman. "What is her name?"

"Amara. It means 'grace' in our language."

"What is your language?"

"It is Igbo." Tomás paused. "And what is yours?"

"Spanish."

Tomás cracked a smile. "Then we are speaking a language that is twisting both our tongues."

I smiled back. "Yes. We are."

Tomás put his finger to his lips. "Listen now. Amara is telling a story."

"But I do not understand your language."

Tomás glanced at me. "Do not worry. What you do not understand, I will explain."

The night was dark, with only a sliver of moon surrounded by a myriad of stars. Here and there, fireflies flickered around us like tiny pinpricks of light. I smelled the salt of the nearby ocean and the sweet fragrance of flowers. I heard the screech of birds and the skittering of small animals in the undergrowth.

The youngest children sat at Amara's feet or lay on their stomachs, elbows on the ground, chins in their hands.

Amara sat on a low stool. Her face was lit by the glow from the fire. She leaned forward and began to speak. The children clapped.

"It is the story about the monkey and the bushcat[14]," Tomás whispered.

Everyone moved closer to Amara. She spoke in a quiet but powerful voice. I didn't want to miss a single word, although I would not understand most of it.

Amara spoke again, making motions to show the bushcat hunting, looking all around but not catching anything. She stopped and rubbed her belly. Then she lay down on the ground and started to scratch and scratch.

Next, she changed her movements to look like a monkey walking by with its arms close to the ground, while it made chattering noises.

Tomás whispered, "Bushcat asks Monkey to pick fleas from her fur. Monkey is not sure but decides to help. Bushcat feels better. She lies down on the ground to sleep."

Amara gazed at us with a knowing look and wagged her finger.

Tomás said, "But you know what monkeys are like."

I nodded along with everyone else.

Amara pretended she was the monkey and tied Bushcat's tail to a tree before running away. The children clapped their hands again.

Bushcat woke up and tried to leave but could not.

Next, Amara curled herself up and moved very slowly.

"What is that?" I asked.

"A snail."

Bushcat made pleading sounds.

"Snail will not help," Tomás said. "He fears Bushcat will kill him. But Bushcat says she will not."

Amara paused in her telling and asked the children a question. Some children nodded their heads; others shook theirs.

Amara picked up a cup of water that was sitting on the ground near her stool. She drank deeply. She showed how the snail untied Bushcat. Amara smiled and spoke a few words. Everyone burst out laughing.

"What is so funny?" I asked.

Tomás could barely speak through his laughter. "She made a joke of how fast a snail can hurry."

It felt good to laugh along with everyone else.

Bushcat traveled home with a big smile on her face. Amara spoke a lot of words that I didn't understand.

"What is she saying now?" I whispered.

"Bushcat makes a plan to take revenge on Monkey. She pretends she is dead. All the animals dance around her. Even Monkey."

Now Amara leaned forward suddenly. The children gasped and their jaws dropped. They all asked questions at the same time.

"What are they saying? Did Bushcat catch Monkey?"

Amara shook her head and pointed up into the tree. She drained the cup of water and then she looked into the faces of her listeners and finished the story.

"That is why Monkey lives in trees," Tomás said. "He is always afraid Bushcat will catch him."

The story was over. The youngest children had fallen asleep. I shuffled off to my pallet in the hut. Before I fell into a deep sleep, I wondered, *Are we like the monkey? Always afraid to come down to the ground? Always afraid to…?*

Chapter 16

"*Incêndio!*" The cry startled me out of my sleep. For a moment, I didn't know where I was. I sprang up and shook the others who were still fast asleep. "Fire!" I slipped into my shoes and rushed out the door of the hut.

A huge fire was racing through the dry stubble. Already, the farthest fields had been consumed. The fire was approaching fast, whipped by a strong wind. Great clouds of smoke stung my eyes and burned my throat. I felt like an animal, stunned by light, frozen where I stood.

Dom Ortiz rushed past us. "Hurry, you fools!" he shouted. "Grab whatever vessel you can! To the river!" His eyes were wild and his hair was blowing every which way. "I'll go to the main house to warn the captain and his wife!"

Amara was standing outside her hut with her soup pot in her arms. I rushed back into the hut and grabbed my bowl. I looked at it and then back at the fire. I almost laughed. It would be like scooping up the sea with a sieve. Then I remembered the copper vessels we had used to make the sugar.

"To the sugar house!" I yelled. We rushed to the house but the door was locked and barred.

I looked around but could not find anything to pry the lock open with. I felt the heat of the fire on my neck and back. I put my shirt up to my face, but my eyes burned from the heat and smoke.

"Tomás, help me!" I shouted as my friend came up to me.

"What should we do?"

"We have to break down that door and get the big pots!"

"We can't! It's too strong!"

"We have to try!"

Tomás stood still, his hands on his hips. "I do not want to help these men who have made us slaves."

"This is no time to talk about that!" I said. "We have to save this place. To save ourselves."

Tomás called to several African men. Together we pushed and pushed until we managed to break down the door. We rushed inside and grabbed whatever pot or pan we could find—these things had been the instruments of our brutal labor, but now they might be used to save us.

"To the river!" I cried. "We must make a line, fill the pots, and put out the fire. Or at least," I gasped, "stop it from spreading."

We rushed down to the river, but then stopped in our tracks. My heart pounded in my ears. Which was worse? The fire or the crocodiles?

"Come on!" I shouted. "We have to try!"

The African men and women, the convicts Antonio and Francisco, even Friar Escobar formed into a line. We scooped water from the river and handed the filled containers from one person to the other.

"Forget the fields!" Dom Ortiz cried over the crackle of flames. "Save the settlement!"

We worked and we worked. My arms felt like lead; my eyes were seared by the heat; my feet felt melted to the ground. It was as if I were breathing fire, not air.

Finally, when the red sun rose over the trees, a heavy rain began to fall. We dropped our containers and collapsed onto the ground.

Friar Escobar stood before us, his arms outstretched to the sky. "Praise the Lord! God's grace has fallen upon us!"

Tendrils of smoke rose from the fields. I coughed up gray spit. My hair was plastered to my scalp; my shirt to my back. I wept from relief and exhaustion.

I looked up then and saw what was left of the settlement. The chapel was destroyed. The sugar house, along with the precious loaves of sugar, was a blackened ruin. Our huts were gone, like scraps of food devoured by a hungry beast. Only Dom Pereira's house and Captain Caminha's house were left standing. They were built of stone and had thus withstood the flames.

I felt a tap on my shoulder.

"Joseph?"

I turned around. "Gracia!" I grabbed Gracia and hugged her tightly. We were both crying and laughing and talking at the same time. "Are you...are you all right?" I croaked.

I hadn't seen Gracia for a long time. She had been confined to the house and had not been allowed to mix with the rest of us. She was wearing the underdress she must have been sleeping in when the alarm was sounded. Over it, she had thrown a worn shawl. Her dark hair hung in a braid down her back. Her face was streaked with soot.

"You're so strong now!" she said.

"And you're taller! Not a little girl anymore."

Gracia blushed. "I've grown up."

"Too fast."

"Yes. Too fast."

We sat on a rock by the river and talked until the sun rose higher in the sky. Ignoring everything that had just happened, ignoring our masters' calls, we talked about Mother and Father, about Trujillo and Lisbon, and eventually about Dom Pereira and Dona Maria.

"I thought I had lost you," I said.

"I was never lost." Gracia smiled. "Maybe just missing for a while."

I grasped Gracia's hands. "We must find a way to meet. I don't want to lose you again." I swallowed hard. "You're the only family I have left." I squeezed more tightly. "Gracia?"

"Yes?"

"If I ever leave this place, you must come with me."

Gracia averted her gaze. "Yes. Probably. Yes."

"What do you mean?"

"I—"

"Gracia?" Dona Maria's voice was shrill. "Gracia, where are you?"

Dona Maria was walking toward us. Her dress was torn in places and her hair was covered with ashes. "What are you doing here, girl?"

"I was just talking to—"

"Never mind." Dona Maria scowled. "Stand up and come with me at once." She put her hand up to her hair. "You must help me wash and then mend my dress. This fire is a catastrophe."

"Yes, mistress." Gracia stood up, wrapped the shawl around her shoulders, and hurried after Dona Maria. She glanced back at me and mouthed the word, "Later."

I wondered when later would be.

Chapter 17

For the rest of the day, I was in a state of shock. Confused. Numb. Along with everyone else, I stumbled through the wreckage of the settlement. We could salvage only a few objects made of metal or stone. The rest had been devoured by the hungry flames.

Our huts were gone. Our pallets were gone. Every scrap of clothing was gone. Amara's stool, on which she had sat to tell stories, was gone. Everything was a drifting pile of ashes. As if our few comforts had never been. We had escaped with our lives, but with only the clothes on our backs.

That night, we sat huddled around the fire. My stomach ached with hunger, my head pounded, my nose was still filled with the acrid smell of smoke. There was little to eat—only a few soggy carrots the women had dug up from their blackened garden. A few knives and machetes had been grabbed in the mad rush to beat back the flames. The men began carving new utensils. Our old wooden bowls and spoons were nothing now but gray cinders.

No music that night. No stories that night. We slept on the hard ground and lay close to each other for warmth and comfort. I heard the whimpers of the younger children, the slap of hands against mosquitoes, the cries of people whose sleep was darkened by nightmares. I couldn't stop shivering, but as the sky began to lighten I dropped off into a restless sleep.

I woke up to Dom Ortiz shaking my shoulder. "Come with me to Captain Caminha's house," he barked. Groggy from lack of sleep, I staggered after him.

When we approached the house, he hissed, "Be quiet unless the captain speaks to you."

He knocked on the door and the captain called, "Enter!"

Captain Caminha's sparkling white shirt was now a dingy gray. He gestured to Dom Ortiz to sit down. I stood against the wall and tried to be invisible.

Dom Ortiz stared at the bench, tested to see if it was solid, and then sat down heavily upon it. He crossed his arms. "What do we do now?" His voice was tight, like a volcano about to erupt. "I came here to run the settlement," he said. "Not to put up with one disaster after another."

The captain shook his head. "Who would have thought when we left Lisbon that we would be faced with so many problems?"

"I knew it would be hard, but this settlement is doomed."

Captain Caminha pounded his fist on the table. Dust and ash rose and settled back down. "Do not say that! We still have hope!"

"Hope?" Dom Ortiz said bitterly. "Where is there hope?" He stood up abruptly and the bench thudded to the ground. "The buildings are in ruin. The fields are scorched. The sugar is gone." He made a quick movement with his head toward me. "And the only one who knows how to make the sugar is…this Jewish boy." He looked at me with disgust and loathing. I flattened myself against the wall.

He stomped toward the door and then turned back to glare at Captain Caminha. "When the next ship arrives from home, I plan to leave on it."

The captain jumped up. "Wait! You can still make your fortune here!"

Dom Ortiz spit on the ground. "Forget it! I have had enough of this cursed island!" With these words, he strode out of the house and slammed the door behind him.

Captain Caminha sank back down on his chair. He beckoned to me. "You, Joseph. Come here."

I took a step or two forward. "Yes, captain."

"Closer, boy."

As I walked toward him, I could see new lines etched on his face and his hair streaked with gray—not the gray of ash but the gray of old age and worry. He looked past me with dull, bloodshot eyes. I almost felt sorry for him, but then I remembered what had happened to my friend David on the ship. I gritted my teeth and tried to look at him without giving away how I truly felt.

He took a deep breath and exhaled slowly. "You know how to make the sugar?"

"Yes, captain."

"Can we plant a new crop?" He muttered. "It is our last hope."

"I…I'm not sure," I said. "If we can find some healthy nodes—"

"Nodes? Where would we find them?"

"Nodes are…we'll have to search…but we may be able to plant again." I paused. "But it will take time for the cane to take root and grow. Meanwhile—"

The captain's shoulders sagged. "Meanwhile, we still have to live."

"Yes, sir."

He smiled a twisted smile. "And what we will live on in the meantime, the Lord only knows."

❖

I did not want to help plant a new crop of sugarcane. One part of me thought that if there was no crop, they would not need us anymore. I even fancied that, one day, Captain Caminha would say to me, "You are free now. You may leave and go back to your home and your family." But in my heart, I knew that that was an impossible hope.

I did not want to help, but I knew I would be punished if I did not try. Besides, I worried about what might happen to us if there was no more sugar to plant on the island.

I found a stack of sugar cane nodes piled in a small hut by the river. I cursed Dom Pereira for his foresight in saving them. Captain Caminha ordered the men to make new handles for axes, hoes, and machetes. The brutal work of digging holes and planting the cane began again.

When the next ship arrived from Portugal, it brought fresh supplies of wine, oil, flour, strong rope, cloth, and cooking pots. Gradually, very gradually, we began to rebuild the settlement. But when the ship left, Dom Ortiz was on board.

Captain Caminha became everything to us: master, overseer, judge. When there were disputes among the settlers or the slaves—and there were many—he resolved them. Just as he had been on board his ship, he was now the undisputed head of the enterprise. No one dared argue against him. Even Friar Escobar faded into insignificance beside the domineering will of the captain. Greed and glory seemed more important on the island, even more important than God.

The settlement struggled on. Each time a ship arrived, some settlers left and a few new ones came. More African slaves were brought to work the sugar. We buried countless people who died of toil, of illness, of homesickness. With each burial, I felt my own despair grow.

After three years had passed, the convicts gained their freedom. They lived together with their African women. The captain didn't discourage these unions. In fact, he often said, "Let them breed. It will replace the people we have lost."

More houses were built, more sugarcane planted, and more sugar made. A new manager, Dom João da Silva, was appointed to run the sugar plantation. He had been one of the original settlers and had often taken over when Dom Ortiz was unable to fulfil his duties. He lived in what had been Dom Pereira's house, and later, Dom Ortiz's.

I reached my fifteenth year, and then my sixteenth. I grew stronger and taller; my voice deepened. I was no longer a boy. It was true I had proved myself useful, as I had resolved to be so long ago. I often wondered if I was *too* useful. It seemed I would be a slave on São Tomé forever.

But when the dry season of 1497 arrived, everything changed.

Chapter 18

Captain Caminha was examining the height of the cane in the fields. "The leaves are yellowing at last," he said to me. "It is almost time for the harvest." Perhaps he was lost in thought. Perhaps the bright sunlight blinded him. In any case, Captain Caminha tripped on a rusty hoe that someone had left lying on the ground.

The hoe gashed his ankle and he landed hard on the ground. He took his dirty handkerchief out of his pocket and wrapped it around the wound. When I walked forward to help him, he waved me away.

For the rest of the day, the captain favored his sore leg. He seemed determined to go about his work as if nothing had happened. He barked orders as usual to everyone he met. By the end of the day, he could barely walk.

When the sun began to set, he beckoned to me. "Joseph! Come here!"

I hurried to his side.

His face was pale. Beads of sweat stood out on his forehead.

"Help me get home." He laid a hand on my shoulder and began to limp toward his house. I could barely stand upright due to his weight. I led him to his chair in the sitting room and he sank into it. "Get me some water," he gasped, "or better still, some wine."

I hurried into the kitchen and found the jug of wine. It was almost empty, but I poured the dregs into a cup. A fly buzzed on the surface. I pinched it between my thumb and forefinger and flicked the dead body to the ground.

When I returned to the sitting room, Captain Caminha was slouched in his chair. "Sir?" I walked closer to him. "Here's your wine."

"Wha...what?" He glanced up at me.

"Wine, sir."

He grasped the cup between shaking hands and downed the contents in a few gulps. He tried to put the cup down, but it clattered to the ground.

I picked it up.

"Leave it, boy," he said. "Help me to my bed. And then go find my wife."

I rushed to the wash house where Dona Maria was busy supervising several African women. One was churning the laundry with a large wooden mallet in a huge tub of hot, soapy water; another rinsed the clothes and wrung them out; a third hung them on strong lines strung between the trees.

Dona Maria stood with her hands on her hips, a scowl on her face. "You are too slow, you lazy good-for-nothings!" She walked from one woman to another, beating the backs of the women with a heavy stick as she passed each one.

The heat, the steam, the smell of the strong soap—all made me dizzy. I grabbed the doorpost of the wash house.

After I had steadied myself, I edged up to the captain's wife. "Dona Maria?"

She spun around and raised her stick, as if to strike me. "What is it?"

I took a step back. "I…I am sorry." I hung my head and licked my dry lips. "My master asked me…you must come at once."

As I looked up, I saw a slight softening in her eyes. "Where? Why?"

"He is in the house. He has had an accident."

Dona Maria swatted my head. "Stupid boy! Why didn't you say so at once?" She wiped her hands on her apron and turned toward the house. "What are you waiting for? Come along!"

When we entered the bedroom, Dona Maria leaned over her husband and said, "How are you feeling, Álvaro?"

Captain Caminha opened his eyes slightly and tried to sit up. "I'm fine. Don't worry about me. Just need to rest." He sank back down against the pillow and closed his eyes.

Dona Maria glared at me. "Get out of here, you worthless boy!"

I was just about to leave when she added, "Come back tomorrow morning."

The next morning, Captain Caminha's condition had worsened. Dona Maria's hair was a tangled mess; dark circles had appeared under her eyes. It looked as if she had slept in her dress.

Dona Maria grabbed my arm. "Find Gracia. Tell her to bring hot water." I started to leave, but then she grabbed my arm again. "And get Antonio, the barber. Hurry!"

"But...where is Gracia?"

"Probably in the kitchen. Go!"

I ran to the back of the house. Gracia was chopping some vegetables. She looked up, startled. "Joseph? What are you doing here?"

"No time to explain," I gasped. "Dona Maria wants hot water. I have to find Antonio!"

"Wait!"

"No time! Talk later!"

I dashed out of the house and down the dirt road to where the convicts had claimed their parcels of land. Their houses were one story tall, with mud walls and thatched roofs.

Antonio's wife was working outside in her vegetable garden, a baby tied to her back with a wide strip of cloth.

"Where's Antonio?" I panted.

The woman shrugged. "Who knows? The man is everywhere but at home."

"Please! I have to find him!"

The woman gestured vaguely down the road. "Over there. He likes to drink with his friend Francisco."

I hurried from one house to another until I finally found the two men, sitting outside Francisco's house and drinking some vile concoction they called wine.

"Hey, boy." Francisco squinted at me. "What are you doing in the slums?" He drained his cup and poured more from a jug sitting on the ground. "Why are you bothering two friends who're having a drink together?" His words were slurred. His burly frame was going to fat. His crooked nose seemed even more misshapen than when I had first met him.

"Yeah." Antonio smirked. "Don't you know it's *dangerous* around here?"

My legs started to shake, but I managed to say, "The mistress told me to get you."

Antonio grinned, showing his missing teeth. I could smell his foul breath from where I was standing. I tried not to gag.

Antonio took a swig of wine and wiped his mouth with the back of his hand. "Anyway, you didn't say please."

I gritted my teeth. "Please."

Antonio stood up, ruffled my hair with his dirty hand, and sighed. "All right. Since you were so polite."

Antonio took one look at the wound and frowned. It had festered quickly—probably due to the heat and damp. The wound was red and full of pus. I retched and ran out of the house. I vomited into the bushes.

"I can bleed him," Antonio was saying when I came back. "Or, I can cut off his foot."

Dona Maria gasped and put her hand to her heart. "No! You won't do either thing!"

Antonio shrugged. "Give him some wine to ease the pain." He bumped into the doorway and staggered out of the house.

"Idiot!" Dona Maria muttered. The front of her dress was spattered with I knew not what; her eyes had a desperate look to them. "Gracia, come here."

Gracia had been standing in a corner of the room and now edged closer to the bed. "Yes, mistress?"

"We must save my husband. Go get more hot water and cloths." She turned to me. "And you, keep the fire going."

"Dona Maria?" I said.

"What?" she snapped.

"The African woman, Amara. She knows about herbs and healing."

Dona Maria pressed her lips together. "I won't have some African witch in my house!" She pushed me away. "Now go get some wood!"

We did what we were told. We worked together the whole long night and the next day, too. In spite of our efforts, by the next night, Captain Caminha was dead. He was buried in the cemetery—along with hundreds of other people who had died on this foul island.

Chapter 19

From that day forward, Dona Maria wore only black—from head to foot, from neck to wrist. She walked around in a daze, not seeming to care about anyone or anything.

Dom João da Silva took over all of Caminha's duties and privileges, in addition to being manager of the settlement. Shortly after the captain's death, he told everyone to gather at the newly built church. Dona Maria sat in front, with Gracia beside her. The convicts Antonio and Francisco, along with the settlers, sat in the middle.

I stood at the back with the other slaves. We mixed freely by then—the Jewish children who had survived, along with my friend Tomás and the other African slaves.

I tried to get Gracia's attention, but she looked only at her mistress or at the crucifix of Jesus at the front. She kept fingering the cross around her neck. My head ached. I wondered why she held onto it so tightly.

Every time I looked at the crucifix, shivers ran up and down my spine. It was carved out of rough wood and its hands and feet were painted red. I shut my eyes tight, not wanting to look at the figure any more than I had to.

"Quiet, everyone!" Dom João da Silva shouted. "Quiet down!"

A hush descended upon the room.

Dom da Silva held up a piece of paper. "I hold here the last will and testament of Captain Álvaro Caminha," he began. "I called you all here because it affects some of you directly."

Dona Maria was sobbing quietly. I almost felt sorry for her.

He began to read. "In the name of God, amen. This document testifies that I, Álvaro Caminha, being sick in bed, but having my natural understanding, offer this last will and testament.

"First, I entrust my soul to God, our Lord, who cared for it and redeemed it with his precious blood."

Who is redeemed? I asked myself.

"My body I return to the earth from which it was formed.

"Item. I order that if God wishes to take me, I wish to be buried in the cemetery behind the church on the island of São Tomé. It is here that I suffered but perhaps achieved some small degree of success.

"Item. I name as the executors of my estate Dom João da Silva and Dona Maria Inês Gil Caminha.

"Item. I declare that I do not remember that I owe any person anything, and I declare this to relieve my conscience.

"Item. I declare that the convict Francisco owes me three cruzados which I lent to him—"

Francisco stood up and shouted, "That's a bloody lie!"

"Please, Francisco," Dom da Silva said. "We shall discuss this later."

"Like hell we will!" yelled Francisco. He stormed out of the church and slammed the door. Antonio followed closely behind him.

Dom da Silva shook his head.

"Item. I leave fifty cruzados to the church on the island of São Tomé. I wish that ten Masses be said for my soul at this humble church which has meant so much to me during these years on the island."

Friar Escobar reddened and bowed his head. His robe seemed much too big for him. He pulled on his collar, as if he couldn't breathe. He kept swatting the flies that were buzzing around his face. He seemed to be muttering a prayer—or perhaps he was just talking to himself.

"Item. Because we have no son or daughter, I leave to my dear wife, Maria Inês Gil Caminha, my house and everything inside it. To her I also leave the bulk of my estate, including 500 cruzados in cash. She may also keep any jewels, clothing, and personal items in her possession."

One of the slaves murmured, "What does this have to do with me?"

"I've got to get to work," said another.

I had heard enough. I wanted to leave, too. The odor of too many people packed too close together was suffocating. But I could not leave. I would be punished, I knew.

Dom da Silva raised his hand until it was quiet again. "Let me continue. You shall see in a moment why I have called you all here."

He squinted at the paper. "During these last years on São Tomé, I have come to a better understanding of the sins I have committed during my life. I wish to meet my Maker with a clear conscience."

Dom da Silva stared at Gracia and then at me. He cleared his throat. "'I therefore grant,'" he cleared his throat again, "'freedom to the slaves, Joseph Belifonte and Gracia Belifonte.'"

I gasped. The room began to spin. I leaned against the wall. I could scarcely breathe. Gracia was a blur. *Freedom? Could it be true?*

Everyone around me began talking at the same time.

"Why do they get to be free, and not us?" a Jewish boy said.

"Does he think he's so special?" said another boy as he glared at me.

"Joseph is always bossing us around," said a third. "He thinks he's better than us."

One Jewish girl was crying. "I want to be free too."

"Leave him alone," Ephraim said. "It's not his fault." He paused. "Joseph only did what he had to do. To survive. Like all of us."

I grasped Ephraim's hand briefly and then made my way slowly down the center aisle. I sat down beside Gracia. She was staring fixedly ahead at the crucifix, as if she were in a daze. Dona Maria sniffed and moved away from us.

"Gracia?" I said. "Look at me."

She turned her head and only then did I see the tears running down her face. "Is it true? Is it really true?"

"It seems to be." I put my arm around her shoulders and she put her head against my chest. I could feel her body shaking.

"Now we can go back home," I said. "Now we can find Mother and Father."

"Yes, but—"

"I shall continue." Dom da Silva wiped his face with his handkerchief. I tried to attend to his words through the pounding of my heart.

"They have served me and my wife well." Here Dom da Silva paused. "For their faithful service, I therefore release them from the bonds of servitude. To each one, I give twenty cruzados. From this day forward, they are free. They may stay on the island or leave—whatever they wish.

"Signed on this 14th day of July, in the year 1497." Dom da Silva looked up from the paper. "That is all. May God have mercy on the soul of Captain Álvaro Caminha."

I watched him fold the paper. *Such a small piece of paper for such a great change.*

Thus, in one moment, my life was transformed.

"Do you truly wish to leave the island?" Dom da Silva and I were standing by the cane fields early the next morning. The birds filled the air with their song; the crickets with their chirping. All around me, the island teemed with life.

"Yes, sir. I do." In spite of the sun beating down on my head, I shivered. *Will this man try to stop me?*

"And your sister? Will she go with you?"

I swallowed hard. Gracia and I had argued after the reading

of the will. She was determined to stay on the island, at least for another six months. She wanted to stay with Dona Maria to help settle her affairs. "She...she has not decided," I said.

Dom da Silva gazed at the high stalks of cane. "Will you not, at least, stay until the cane is harvested and the sugar is made?" He frowned. "We have no other person who knows so well how to make the sugar. It will also give me time to find someone else."

I shook my head. "I shall stay until the next ship arrives from Portugal. I plan to be on it."

Dom da Silva sighed. "There is nothing I can do to persuade you?"

"Nothing."

"And when you get back to Lisbon, what will you do?"

I balled my hands into fists. "I will search for my parents."

"And if you do not find them?"

"If they are not in Lisbon, then I shall keep searching." I couldn't look him in the eyes. "Until I find out where they are—alive or dead. Until I know what happened to them." I swallowed hard. "And they know what happened to us."

"All right, young man," Dom da Silva said. "You are free now. I cannot stop you."

Chapter 20

A month later, when the *São Lucas* arrived from Portugal, I booked passage on it. These words sound so simple to say, but it was a hard thing to do.

Although I had often cursed the island and the wretched fate that had brought me to it, still I had somehow survived and grown to manhood. I had almost become used to the life here.

On the evening before I was to leave, I sat with Tomás near the fire. "You understand why I must leave?"

"Yes, Joseph. A person must find his home." He looked sideways at me. "How do you say it? A place in the world."

I put my hand on his shoulder. "I hope that one day you too will be free." I pressed harder. "That you will find *your* place in the world."

He smiled. "I hope so, my friend."

I reached into my pocket and pulled out one of Dom Pereira's books. "This is for you."

Tomás blushed. "Really? For me?"

"Now you can practice your reading and writing."

"Thank you, my friend." He looked around, as if to be sure we were alone. "One gift deserves another. Now I will tell you my real name." He put his mouth close to my ear and whispered his name.

"Thank you for your gift," I said.

"And thank you for yours."

It was much harder to say good-bye to Gracia.

We were walking along the shore. I could smell the tang of salt and fish in the air. "I don't understand," I said. "Don't you want to go back home? Don't you want to find Mother and Father?"

She stopped in her tracks and looked down at the ground. "I can scarcely remember them. They seem like phantoms; like a dream." She clutched the cross that hung from her neck. "I have a new life here with Dona Maria."

I frowned. "You hang on to that cross as if it's the doll you lost a long time ago." I reached out and tried to yank it off her neck. "Can't you see? It won't save you!"

She pushed my hand away and turned her back to me. "Go away, Joseph. Leave me alone." Her shoulders were shaking.

I tried again. "But you've seen how cruel Dona Maria is to her slaves!" I said. "How can you stay with someone like that?"

Gracia gazed out to sea. "Since the captain died, she has been kinder to me. She needs me." She glanced at me over her shoulder. "Besides, I have my faith."

I could hear the waves crash against the shore. I felt my heart breaking, too. "But you're Jewish!" I grabbed her arm and forced her to turn around.

Gracia stared at me and put her hands on her hips. "No longer. I believe in Jesus Christ. He was the Son of God. He died for our sins."

I put my hands on her shoulders and shook her. "No! You can't believe what Friar Escobar has been preaching!"

Gracia shook my hands off her shoulders. "But I do." She sighed. "Besides, even if I went back with you and even if we found Mother and Father, they would never accept me. Not while I'm a Christian." She lowered her head and spoke more softly. "No. I can never go back."

She stood up straighter. "Joseph, you must go your own way now. And you must let me go mine."

My throat tightened and I could scarcely speak. Tears were flowing down her cheeks, as they were down mine.

"Then let me bless you," I said, "the way Father used to bless us."

Gracia looked up at me through wet eyes and nodded.

I put my hand on her head. "May God bless you and protect you. May God's presence shine upon you and be gracious unto you. May God's presence be with you and grant you peace."

We embraced. Then we parted. I knew I would probably never see my sister again.

The next morning, I gathered my few possessions and boarded the ship. As we departed, I gazed back at the island of São Tomé—the place where I had suffered so much misery. The sun shimmered on the wet leaves of the jungle. The raucous cries of parrots and the buzzing of insects filled the air.

As the wind billowed the sails, I watched the foam flowing in the ship's wake. I gripped the wooden railing and felt the spray of saltwater on my face.

I did not know what awaited me. I only knew that the past was an ocean of tears. A great longing grew inside me. I would return to Lisbon to search for my parents. If I could not find them there, I would journey to Antwerp.

Somewhere in this world, I would find a home at last. And on the doorpost of that home, I would fasten a mezuzah.

Endnotes

1. Quoted from *Expulsion 1492 Chronicles* in Delores Sloan, *The Sephardic Jews of Spain and Portugal: Survival of an Imperiled Culture in the Fifteenth and Sixteenth Centuries* (Jefferson, North Carolina: McFarland & Company, 2009), 14.

2. Quoted from the *Edict of Expulsion* in Erna Paris, *From Tolerance to Tyranny: A Cautionary Tale from Fifteenth Century Spain* (Toronto: Cormorant Books, 2015), 231.

3. The number of Jews living in Spain in 1492 varies widely according to different sources. Some say 200,000; others, 40,000. Whatever the real number, it will not affect the story I am about to tell.

4. It's difficult to determine the modern-day equivalent of this amount. One source states that a physician's annual salary in those days would have been about eight cruzados.

5. The number of children taken varies according to different sources—700 to 5,000.

6. Deuteronomy, 6:4-6.

7. Quoted in Paris, 295: Judeo-Spanish ballad, "El paso del Mar Rojo".

8. Lyrics sung by Hadass Pal-Yarden, https://www.youtube.com/watch?v=qcsXH0Uv-vE, viewed Jan. 28/17.

9. The common term for dysentery.

10. The term "negro" was not used in a negative sense in those days. "Homem negro" was the Portuguese word for "African" or "black man".

11. This illness was malaria, common to the island of São Tomé. The word "malaria" comes from the Italian, "mal aria", meaning "bad air". The disease is caused by parasites and is spread by mosquitoes.

12. Lyrics sung by Hadass Pal-Yarden, https://www.youtube.com/watch?v=qcsXH0Uv-vE, viewed Jan. 28/17, May 4/17.

13. Nathan Goldberg, *Passover Haggadah*, Hoboken, NJ: Ktav, 1993, 13.

14. Adapted from "Why Monkeys Live in Trees", retold by Roger D. Abrahams, *African Folktales*, (Pantheon Books, 1983), 156.

Author's Note

This story has been painful to write. If I have done any justice to the subject, it will be a painful book to read. There is no way around this, nor should there be. I wrote this book to bring to light one of the most horrific events in Jewish history, as well as to tell a story of slavery in the late medieval period. When the Jews were expelled from Spain, only one day before Christopher Columbus set out on his first journey to the "New World," a cross-current of history took place that would send ripples down through the centuries.

One of our tasks as citizens of the twenty-first century is to learn from the past. I hope this novel will, at least in small part, add to our knowledge and understanding.

Glossary

bloody flux: dysentery

carrack: a type of three-masted ship

cruzado: a form of Portuguese currency

degredados: convicts (Portuguese)

gato de nueve colas: "cat of nine tails," whip (Spanish)

gracias: thank you (Spanish)

hashkabah: Sephardic Jewish prayer recited at the funeral or on the anniversary of a person's death

incêndio: fire (Portuguese)

juderia: the Jewish quarter in a Spanish or Portuguese town or city

matzah: unleavened bread eaten by Jews during the eight days of Passover

mezuzah: a piece of parchment within a case inscribed with specific Hebrew verses from the Bible

mitzvah: a commandment; a good deed (Hebrew)

obrigado: thank you (Portuguese)

papagaio: parrot (Portuguese)

por favor: please (Portuguese)

seder: the ritual feast that marks the beginning of the Jewish holiday of Passover. It involves a retelling of the story of the liberation of the Israelites from slavery in ancient Egypt

sesmarias: land grants (Portuguese)

Shema Israel: "Hear, O Israel," the first words of the credo of Jewish faith (Hebrew)

thwart: a seat extending across a boat

Further Reading: Fiction

* for young adults

- * Fox, Paula. *The Slave Dancer*. New York: Atheneum, 2001 (1973).
- * Gidwitz, Adam. *The Inquisitor's Tale: Or, The Three Magical Children and Their Holy Dog*. New York: Dutton, 2016.
- * Greene, Jacqueline Dembar. *The Secret Shofar of Barcelona*. Minneapolis: Kar-Ben, 2009.
- * Lester, Julius. *The Old African*. Illus. by Jerry Pinkney. New York: Dial, 2005.
- * Little, Melanie. *The Apprentice's Masterpiece: A Story of Medieval Spain*. Toronto: Annick Press, 2008.
- * Williams, Sheron. *Imani's Music*. Illus. by Jude Daly. New York: Atheneum, 2002.

Further Reading: Non-Fiction

* for young adults

- Abbott, Elizabeth. *Sugar: A Bittersweet History*. Toronto: Penguin, 2008.
- Aronson, Marc and Marina Budhos. *Sugar Changed the World: A Story of Magic, Spice, Slavery, Freedom, and Science*. New York: Clarion, 2010.
- Caldeira, Arlindo Manuel. "Learning the Ropes in the Tropics: Slavery and the Plantation System on the Island of São Tomé." *African Economic History* 39 (2011): 35-71.
- * Gann, Marjorie and Janet Willen. *Five Thousand Years of Slavery*. Toronto: Tundra, 2011.
- * Grant, Reg. *Slavery: Real People and Their Stories of Enslavement*. London: Dorling Kindersley, 2009.
- Greenfield, Sidney M. "Plantations, Sugar Cane and Slavery." *Roots and Branches: Current Directions in Slave Studies* (Summer/Eté, 1979): 85-119.
- Heuman, Gad and Trevor Burnard (eds.) *The Routledge History of Slavery*. London: Routledge, 2011.

- Hodges, Tony and Malyn Newitt. *Sao Tome and Principe: From Plantation Colony to Microstate*. Boulder, Colorado: Westview Press, 1988.
- * Lester, Julius. *From Slave Ship to Freedom Road*. Illus. by Rod Brown. New York: Penguin, 1998.
- Libé, Moshé (ed.) with Norman Simms. *Jewish Child Slaves in São Tomé: papers, essays, articles, and original documents related to the July 1995 conference*. Wellington, NZ: New Zealand Chronicle Publications, 2003.
- * Mann, Charles C. *1493 For Young People: From Columbus's Voyage to Globalization*. New York: Seven Stories Press, 2014.
- Paris, Erna. *From Tolerance to Tyranny: A Cautionary Tale from Fifteenth Century Spain*. Toronto: Cormorant Books, 2015. (originally published as *The End of Days*, Toronto: Lester Publishing, 1995).
- Rediker, Marcus. *The Slave Ship: A Human History*. New York: Penguin, 2007.
- Schama, Simon. *The Story of the Jews: Finding the Words: 1000 BCE–1492 CE*. Toronto: Allen Lane, 2014.
- Simms, Norman. "Jewish Children of São Tomé". Simmsdownunder.blogspot.com. Posted 17 May 2013.
- Smith, Andrew F. *Sugar: A Global History*. London: Reaktion Books, 2015.
- Walvin, James. *A Short History of Slavery*. London: Penguin, 2006.

Websites

- Free the Slaves (U.S.) www.freetheslaves.net
- Anti-Slavery International (England) www.antislavery.org
- Alliance Against Modern Slavery (Canada)
  https://www.girlsnotbrides.org/members/
  alliance-against-modern-slavery/

YouTube

- Prof. Jane Gerber and Prof. Paulo Mendes Pinto. "The Portuguese Jewish Legacy". Published July 3, 2013. Viewed December 2, 2016.
- Julius Lester. "To Be a Slave." Published January 31, 2015. Viewed March 8, 2017.

Acknowledgments

Friends and family along the way: Meryl Arbing, Max Dublin, Toby Dublin, Michael Greenstein, Teme Kernerman, Myrna Levy, Tina Natale, David Nitkin, Marylyn Peringer, Marilyn Potter, Judy Saul, Saul and Vivienne Ship, Sheryn Weber, and Connie Zwingerman

The talented and insightful women in my writers' group, who helped me flesh out this book, chapter by chapter, month after month: Rona Arato, Sydell Waxman, Lynn Westerhout, Frieda Wishinsky

Ilya Slavutskiy, Reference Services Librarian, Center for Jewish History, New York City

Dr. Gabriel Mordoch, Judaica and Western European Language Cataloger, University of Michigan, Ann Arbor, Michigan

Norman Simms, retired scholar, Hamilton, New Zealand

Rabbi Rifat Sonsino, PhD, Rabbi Emeritus, Temple Beth Shalom, Needham, MA

Rabbi Don Splansky, Rabbi Emeritus, Temple Beth Am, Framingham, MA

Rabbi Yael Splansky, Senior Rabbi, Holy Blossom Temple, Toronto.

Once again, I'm blessed to work with the amazing women at Second Story Press: Allie Chenoweth, Kathryn Cole, Emma Rodgers, Ellie Sipila, and Phuong Truong. Thanks to Carolyn Jackson, editor extraordinaire, who helped smooth out the rough parts to make a more cohesive whole. Thanks to Sue Todd for her creativity in producing the cover and map art. Most of all, I'm grateful to Margie Wolfe, who time after time has demonstrated her faith in my writing. From one DP kid to another, I offer my heartfelt thanks.

I am grateful to be supported by Toronto Arts Council with funding from the City of Toronto. I would also like to thank the Ontario Arts Council for their support.

About the Author

Anne Dublin is the award-winning author of biographies and historical novels for young people. Anne's latest book, *44 Hours or Strike!* received the Canadian Jewish Literary Award (Youth) in 2016. A retired teacher-librarian, Anne spends her time reading, writing, singing in a choir, playing recorder, folk dancing, and swimming. Anne lives in Toronto, Canada.